PUFFIN BOOKS

Playing it Cool

Jacqueline Roy is a lecturer in Black and Women's Literature and Creative Writing at the Manchester Metropolitan University. Her books for young adults include *Soul Daddy* and *King Sugar*.

Other books by Jacqueline Roy

A DAUGHTER LIKE ME
FAT CHANCE

Jacqueline Roy

Playing It Cool

PUFFIN BOOKS

PUFFIN BOOKS

Published by the Penguin Group
Penguin Books Ltd, 27 Wrights Lane, London W8 5TZ, England
Penguin Putnam Inc., 375 Hudson Street, New York, New York 10014, USA
Penguin Books Australia Ltd, Ringwood, Victoria, Australia
Penguin Books Canada Ltd, 10 Alcorn Avenue, Toronto, Ontario, Canada M4V 3B2
Penguin Books (NZ) Ltd, Cnr Rosedale and Airborne Roads, Albany,
Auckland, New Zealand

Penguin Books Ltd, Registered Offices: Harmondsworth, Middlesex, England

First published by Viking 1997
Published in Puffin Books 1998
5 7 9 10 8 6 4

The moral right of the author has been asserted

Set in Bembo

Made and printed in England by Clays Ltd, St Ives plc

British Library Cataloguing in Publication Data
A CIP catalogue record for this book is available from the British Library

ISBN 0-140-38183-X

For Kayum Roy, with love

One

I was sitting on a draughty station concourse with my mother, waiting for my gran to come. She was already twenty minutes late.

'You will be good for Gran, won't you, Grace?' Mum said.

I considered it. Well, I might, but then again, I might not. It depended on a lot of things. I didn't see why I had to stay with Gran in the first place. I wanted to go on travelling around with Mum. But now Mum had decided that I needed to be settled somewhere, get a good education, not a bit of this and a bit of that in whatever country she happened to be working at any given moment.

I'd argued, of course. I'd always got on well with Mum. She was special. She was an opera singer and had worked in every major city in the world. Up until then, I'd travelled with her, living in hotels or rented apartments. Mum and I had always stuck together, ever since she and my dad had split up when I was three. I seldom thought about him; we lost contact ages back, so Mum was the most important person in my universe.

'I don't want to go,' I said for the umpteenth time.

Mum sighed. 'I only want what's best for you.'

'What's best for me is staying with you.'

'It's only for a few months and then we'll think again.'

Suddenly, I was frightened. 'I will live with you once this trip's over, won't I? You won't make me stay with Gran for always?'

'No,' she promised. 'Trust me, Grace. I only want what's best for you.'

'I wish you'd stop saying that,' I said.

I felt like an unwanted parcel, shunted back and forth as the grown-ups decided. I didn't want to live with Gran, I didn't even know her; the travelling had meant that I'd only seen her once or twice and I'd been very little then.

As if she knew what I was thinking, Mum said, 'You used to love your gran. She's quite a character. You said she played the most wonderful games with you the last time you saw her. Do you remember?'

I stared into space. 'I remember some things about her. She told amazing stories, and she didn't get tired of playing, not like most grown-ups.'

'And you remember liking her?'

'I did like her, Mum, but it was a long time ago.'

She sighed. 'I know,' she said. 'I should have tried to see Mother more often. Then this wouldn't seem so strange to you.'

I nodded. Although I wasn't happy at the prospect, and I wouldn't have admitted it for anything, I was aware that there might be a good side to staying with my gran. Much as I loved travelling with Mum,

I'd often thought it would be nice to lead an ordinary existence, stay in one place for a while, live like a member of a normal family. I was even looking forward to going to just one school. Up until then, I'd been to dozens, staying in each for just a few weeks at a time. Or else I'd been taught on my own by one of the many tutors hired by my mother.

I thought over what I knew about Gran. She'd been brought to England from Jamaica years and years ago when she'd been a lot younger than me. She'd been married, but her husband, my grandfather, had died about eighteen months ago. She did some kind of writing for a living. She'd even been on television once, talking about growing up, but I'd missed the programme; we'd been in New York when it had gone out.

I barely remembered what Gran looked like. How could you start living with someone you didn't really know? Would I be allowed to watch my favourite television programmes? Would I be made to go to bed early every night? What sort of food would I have to eat? Would Gran cope with the fact that I hated most vegetables, but especially carrots, or would carrots be served at every meal? What sort of room would I sleep in? Would the house be big enough? I was going to live in a place I'd never even seen. My wish for an ordinary life was swamped by all these worries. If only this big tour wasn't coming up, and if only I wasn't nearly twelve. What was it about nearing twelve that made everyone so anxious about your future?

Mum put her hand on my shoulder. 'Here she is,' she said, and then she began to walk towards a small African-Caribbean woman with a weight problem and no taste in clothes. She was in a bright green pair of trousers and a huge orange jacket with a rainbow-coloured scarf. But I was most aware of her feet; she was wearing silver glitter ankle boots.

Gran hugged Mum and wiped away a tear from her cheek. Then she half-walked, half-ran towards me, uttering this strange, high-pitched squeal of excitement. I cringed. I tried to scrunch up small as I sat on the suitcase, in order to hide myself, but Gran kept on coming like a brightly coloured tank, her arms outstretched. I was clasped in a tight embrace. 'Hello, Gran,' I said, my voice muffled by Gran's bulk.

'This is a happy, happy day,' said Gran, releasing me slowly and beaming.

'Yes,' I muttered.

'How long is it since I've seen you? Must be eight, nine years. Odette, why have you kept her from me all this time?'

'I'm sorry, Mum, you know how it's been. One place after another and hardly a breathing space between.'

'No life for a child,' said Gran, and I frowned.

'What about something to eat?' said Mum. 'We've got some time. My flight doesn't leave until this evening.'

'Couldn't you stay just one night?' I asked.

Mum put her arm around me. 'You know what we agreed. No long goodbyes, no fuss. And I really do have to be on that plane, or I'll miss tomorrow's dress rehearsal.'

I nodded, but I was cross. I didn't remember agreeing to anything, she'd decided it all, and the no fuss idea was hers not mine. I wanted as much fuss as possible if she was going to leave me.

'Where do you want to eat? Let's make this a real treat.'

Gran said, 'I know a good place, an American diner. Let's go there.'

'I thought I was choosing,' I said in a small voice, but Gran didn't hear, she was waddling off through the station in hot pursuit of the diner.

We took a taxi. All through the journey, Gran chatted about what she'd been doing lately. She seemed to lead a busy life, visiting friends and going to concerts.

'Have you ever seen Mum sing?' I asked.

'I used to go when she was young, but it's not really my bag, you know. I'm a reggae woman. And rap, of course. And a bit of jungle.'

Mum laughed. 'You don't change, Mother,' she said.

'Now why would I want to change?' Gran answered.

I stared out of the window. Gran was making it up. No one of more than fifty really liked that sort of music. Then I remembered the ankle boots, and began to think that anything was possible.

The diner was crowded, but Gran found us a corner table. Mum pushed me into the seat next to Gran which annoyed me because I'd wanted to sit beside her instead. Gran hogged the menu but then a waitress came and gave us a couple more. 'Hello, nice to see you again,' she said to Gran. It was obvious that she was a regular customer.

'This is my daughter and granddaughter.'

'Pleased to meet you,' said the waitress. 'Are you ready to order?'

'I'll have a half-pound cheeseburger with fries and a chocolate shake. Don't bother with the salad, darling, I'll only leave it. Oh, and I'll have a Coke as well. And I could start with some onion rings.' Gran closed her menu with a satisfied smile. 'What about you, Grace? Odette?'

'I don't think I can put away a half-pounder,' Mum replied. 'I'll just have a Caesar salad, I think. And iced water.'

'Onion rings for you too?'

Mum shook her head. 'What do you want, Grace?'

I ordered a plain, regular burger.

'Quite right,' said Gran. 'You don't want to get too stuffed. Their puddings are a heavenly experience.'

Watching Gran eat was a revelation. No wonder she was on the tubby side. She smothered her fries in ketchup and gorged the burger like it was her last-ever meal. Trails of onion descended down her chin.

The waitress took our plates. 'Was everything all right?' she said.

Gran's cleared plate seemed to suggest that it had been. One good thing, if Gran didn't like salad, she probably wouldn't like carrots much either, so at least I wouldn't be force-fed watery veg during my visit.

Gran asked for the dessert menu. 'Are you sure?' asked Mum.

'Quite sure,' replied Gran happily.

'Well I'm going to pass, I think,' Mum said.

Gran pored over the menu. 'What's your special?' she asked the waitress.

'Banana cream pie with chocolate sauce.'

Gran shook her head slowly as if unable to take in the magnificence of it. 'And the chocolate fudge cake comes with ice cream?'

The waitress nodded.

'Oh, I can't decide,' said Gran. 'Grace, what are you going for? Maybe I could try some of yours if you get something different.'

'I don't want a pudding,' I said. I was feeling rather sick; it was a combination of a big meal, a lot of travelling and nervousness.

Gran looked shocked. 'But you must,' she said. 'They have the best desserts in London. You really will miss out if you don't at least try one.'

'No, really,' I answered.

'She's not a pudding person, Mum.'

'No?' Gran looked sad. 'I thought all children liked puddings.'

'Don't let it stop you having one,' Mum said.

Gran clearly had no intention of allowing that to happen. She turned her attention back to the menu. 'Well, look, give me two in case Grace changes her mind, or maybe Odette decides to have one. I'll take raspberry cheesecake with cream and the fudge cake with ice cream.'

'I won't change my mind,' I said.

'Then there'll be all the more for me,' Gran answered.

We took another taxi back to the station and Mum prepared to take the train to Gatwick. 'Don't forget,' she said, 'you be good for your gran.'

I nodded. 'And you'll phone me, won't you, all the time?'

'You know I will.'

I pulled her close and whispered in her ear. 'And if I don't like it at Gran's, you'll come and get me, won't you?'

'You'll be just fine,' replied Mum, and, kissing me goodbye, she ran to catch the train.

Two

Alone with Gran, I was suddenly shy. The enormity of being left with someone who was a virtual stranger took hold. I wished Mum hadn't left me. It seemed really cruel of her to dump me.

If Gran knew that I was feeling strange, she certainly didn't show it. 'Come on, darling,' she said briskly. 'No sense letting the grass grow.'

Gran began to walk out of the station with a speed that belied her short legs and stocky build. I realized I was about an inch taller than she was, which seemed odd, but also made me feel grown up – far too grown up to shed tears, I decided. I began to follow Gran towards the bus stop.

Gran thrust her way through the flocks of commuters. Every now and then, she swore loudly as her bag knocked someone's shins or a couple refused to part to let her pass. I was shocked. Swearing was for the young, not for people who were almost old-age pensioners with free bus passes. 'We don't have to rush,' I said, feeling breathless with the effort of trying to keep pace.

'No sense dawdling,' replied Gran. 'It's the early bird that catches the worm.'

I wondered what sort of worm Gran was

intending to catch. She seemed so determined about it. 'Can't we get a taxi?' I asked. I'd been up since five that morning and I was tired.

'No sense wasting good money on taxis when the bus stops outside my door,' Gran answered.

I sighed meaningfully and looked intently at my grandmother as we hurried on. Her Afro hair was mainly grey. Her chest was enormous. Her bottom drooped. And judging by those garish clothes, she had no shame whatsoever. You couldn't choose your relations; your only option was to disown them. I edged back a little way, hoping that passers-by would assume we were two unrelated people merely walking along the same stretch of pavement.

As if she was aware of my critical assessment of her, Gran started to chatter about anything and everything.

'Not so warm today, is it?' she said.

'I wouldn't know. We only flew in this morning. It was warm enough in Italy.'

'I don't know why I came to this cold climate. Give me blue, not all this dull greyness you get all the time.'

'It is grey,' I said, surprised to find that we agreed on something.

'You've grown so much, I hardly recognized you.'

'Children grow. It's an occupational hazard.'

Gran looked bewildered for a moment and then she laughed, a high-pitched shriek that caused heads to turn. 'And you have a sense of humour too! I knew you'd grow up right, I just knew you would!'

'Are we nearly at the bus stop now? It's been a long journey and I'm pretty tired.'

'*Tired?* Kids your age have bags of energy. Your mother, bless her heart, she used to whizz around morning through to night.'

I thought of the elegant, cool and clever woman we'd left behind at Victoria station and wondered how on earth she'd survived being dragged up by this lunatic. She was scientific proof that you could escape your genes, you didn't have to end up like the other crazy members of your family. I remembered my cousin Beverly then and wondered when I'd be seeing her. We hadn't met since we were five, but I'd quite liked her then and I was looking forward to having someone to hang out with. I asked Gran about her and she said, 'Beverly is coming to eat with us tomorrow. I knew you'd want some company your own age, and Beverly doesn't get on so well with the other boys and girls at school. They're always teasing her and things.' Suddenly, she changed the subject. 'You sure you're tired? Only I thought we might go to the shops and then have a little something in a café.'

I felt a brief spark of excitement. I loved shopping. But then I remembered that I'd have to put up with having Gran for company and continue to be seen in public with an elderly, grey-haired, fat, brightly clothed woman with a high-pitched voice. 'I really am tired, Gran,' I said.

Gran looked disappointed and said plaintively, 'I

only have a little bun and cheese in the house. I thought you'd like the café.'

'It's OK, honest. Anyway, we've only just eaten.'

'More than two hours ago!'

'Well, I only eat when I'm hungry and I'm not hungry now.'

'But we could go shopping, couldn't we? It's just that I've seen a little something in a shop and I was planning to fetch it today before they sell out.'

'My bag's really heavy,' I said.

'Then let me take it,' replied Gran.

'No, really.'

'Let me take it, child, it's no trouble to me.' A brief tussle followed, which Gran won. I felt puny by comparison.

'*Please* can we get a taxi?' I asked again.

'I don't have money to burn, you know.'

'I've got money. Mum gave me some. And I've got a savings account with a cash card, so I can withdraw money from those machines.'

'We'll catch the bus,' said Gran firmly. 'And we'll go upstairs so you can see all the London sights.'

The bus came straight away, and I was dragged to the upper deck. Gran grabbed the front seat and put her feet on the ledge just below the window, crossing her ankles so her silver boots were visible to all. I cringed and looked out of the window.

'Look at the river,' Gran shrieked, grabbing me by the arm to get my attention. I stared at the water morosely. London was a writhing, choking mass of dirt and pollution. Who in their right mind would want to live there? I thought of my mother, who in no time at all, would be wandering the streets of Paris. The air was clean (or cleaner than in London) and although the streets were busy, they weren't overcrowded. You could breathe there. All around you, there were green trees and people were sensible and polite, they didn't drag you round on buses and they didn't put their feet where feet weren't meant to be. And most important of all, they acted their age, they didn't pretend to be young when obviously they were only fit for burial.

Gran searched her turquoise and orange velvet bag with tassels hanging down it and pulled out a pack of cigarettes. I nudged her in the ribs. 'You can't, it says "No Smoking". Look!'

'I don't care so much for rules and regulations,' Gran replied. 'Rules are meant to be broken. Didn't anybody ever teach you that?'

I frowned. The idea of being taught to break the rules was an interesting one. Mum had always made sure that I did as I was told. You could talk back from time to time, but you couldn't go too far. 'I want you to be good,' she always said, and she encouraged goodness by teaching me right from wrong. Smoking was definitely in the 'wrong' category. Apart from anything else, it damaged your health. 'Someone will come and tell you off,' I said curtly. 'Anyway, I'm not doing any passive smoking. I don't want to get lung cancer or have my legs cut off.' I remembered the film I'd seen at one of my many schools about all the awful things that happened to people who smoked. It was clear that Gran was heading for a miserable death. At her age, she should have known better.

Gran reluctantly returned the cigarettes to her bag.

'Do you smoke in the house?' I asked her. 'Only I hate the smell and it makes me cough.'

'I could smoke in the yard,' Gran said meekly.

I felt embarrassed. In a way, it was good of Gran to let me stay, I shouldn't have started telling her what to do in her own home. 'Sorry,' I said. 'I didn't mean . . .'

Gran gave another of her beaming smiles. 'I've been thinking I should give it up, you know. It's not a healthy thing. And I could save a lot of money. Come on, up you get. This is our stop.'

We got off the bus outside a shop that was so full of plastic junk that it flowed through the door and on to the pavement. Gran hurried to the furthest container and rummaged inside it. 'It was here yesterday,' she said. 'Beautiful, it was, but I didn't have enough to pay for it until I got some money from the bank.'

'What was it?' I asked, stifling my impatience.

'Well, it was a thing like a . . . you know, one of those cutter things, but pretty, not like usual. I like unusual things, they brighten up the place.'

'Can you be a bit more precise? What cutter things? I mean, what do they cut?'

'Well, they just make the edges fancy, you know?'

'The edges of what?' My patience had left me

now. I was wondering how I'd stand living with anyone so muddled.

'Ah, here it is, found it. Look!'

I looked. It was a round contraption with serrated edges in blue and yellow plastic. It wasn't anything I recognized. 'But what does it do?' I asked.

'Oh, this and that,' said Gran. 'It'll look so cosy in my kitchen, nice it up, it will.'

'I'll take your word for it,' I said under my breath. Then I added, 'Can we go home now? Only I really am tired.'

'You don't want a bit to eat?'

'No, I'm still full from lunch, I told you. Anyway, I want to eat indoors where no one's gawping at us.'

'No one's gawping, Grace. Everyone just getting along with their own business.'

I glanced around me. It was true; nobody was paying us any attention at all. How could they ignore someone like Gran? It seemed impossible.

'London's a big place,' said Gran, as if she were reading my thoughts. 'People just get on, they don't mind you as long as you don't get in their way.'

I was relieved. I'd been afraid that Gran would continue to make such a spectacle of herself that people would queue up to watch. 'Are we going then, Gran?' I asked again.

Gran sighed. 'I was looking forward to a bit of chicken in a café. But all right, if you're tired.' She shook her head, slowly, trying to fathom out how an almost-twelve-year-old could have less stamina than she had.

'Gran –' I began.

'You know, I really don't feel like a gran. Why don't you just call me by my name? It makes me feel old, all this Gran business.'

'All right,' I said wearily, but then I realized I didn't actually know what Gran's name was. She'd always been just Gran, nothing more.

'Patience,' said Gran.

'I'm being as patient as I can!' I snapped in reply.

Gran burst out laughing. The shrieks seemed to echo round the street. 'Patience is my name,' she said at last.

I thought back to all the jostling and pushing and swearing that Gran had done at the station. No one could fit a name like Patience less than Gran did.

'When they christened me, they made a good joke,' said Gran, still laughing. I tried to laugh back, but I felt too miserable. One thing was certain; living with Gran would take a lot more patience than I was ever likely to manage.

Three

The first thing that struck me about Gran's home was how small it was. I'd been expecting something larger than a small terraced house in a backstreet. As I went inside, I became aware of the clutter. Even in the narrow hall, there were cardboard boxes tied up with string. An elderly cat stumbled towards us, mewing piteously. I stiffened; I didn't like cats, I thought they were sharp, cross creatures and the noise they made irritated me.

'That's just Marley,' said Patience. 'Don't mind him, his miaow's worse than his bite.'

'He looks old.'

'He's fifteen. That's quite an age for a cat, isn't it, Marley?' Gran picked him up and nursed him in her arms as if he were a baby. I hoped I wouldn't be expected to mother Marley – he was far too big and probably had fleas.

'Come and sit down, make yourself comfortable,' said Patience as I took off my jacket. She opened the door to the living room and I went in uncertainly.

It was a strange room for a grown-up to have. Everywhere you looked, there were frogs of some description: wooden ones, pottery ones, beanbag frogs, knitted frogs, frogs in frocks, frogs in jeans, frog bookends, frog cushion covers . . . the list was endless. I imagined that when you went crazy, this was the kind of thing you saw. 'Help, doctor, wherever I look there are frogs.'

'What do you think?' asked Patience, with pride in her voice. She obviously wanted an enthusiastic response. 'I collect frogs,' she added needlessly.

'Yes, I could tell,' I replied, struggling to keep sarcasm at bay.

'Every Christmas, every birthday, guess what people send to me?'

'Rabbits?' I asked. It just slipped out.

Patience laughed for a long time. 'I do like a sense of humour,' she said.

'Mum doesn't give you frogs.'

Patience sighed. 'She thinks they're silly,' she said.

I thought Mum had a point, but I didn't say so. After all, I was going to be living in Gran's house. 'You've got multimedia,' I said, looking at Patience's computer.

'Wonderful thing,' said Gran. 'It's changed my life, I'm not joking. It prints six pages a minute, just imagine that, and the graphics you get on the games, they're unbelievable, stunning. Look, I'll show you.'

'Gran –'

'Patience.'

'Yes, sorry, Patience. I'm not really interested in computers.'

'You don't like computers? You don't like the games?'

'They're boring, you repeat the same thing over and over.'

'But that's what's good about them,' answered Gran in bewilderment. 'I mean, the skill is in learning from the repetition, going with it, getting better and better.'

I shrugged. 'To me, they're just boring,' I repeated.

'Don't they teach you anything at school any more?'

I shrugged again, but at least this was a line I understood, and at least it showed that Gran was capable of sounding like a grown-up once in a while. It was a relief.

'Come, I'll show you round the rest of the place.'

I followed apprehensively. Next door there was a dining room which had a pine dresser covered in more frogs: frog jugs, frog mugs.

'Don't you ever get fed up with them?' I asked.

'Fed up with frogs?' asked Gran in surprise, as if the idea was a new one to her.

'I mean, they're everywhere, aren't they?'

'I like them,' said Patience.

'I kind of gathered that,' I said, and again Patience laughed, a rich, full laugh that seemed to fill the house.

'Come upstairs and see your room.'

'Will I like it?' I don't know why I said that. I knew it was a stupid question, but I just couldn't help myself.

Either Gran didn't hear or she didn't think it was worth answering. She bounded up the stairs like a gazelle on a pogo stick, though her bulk spoilt the effect; the house walls appeared to shake.

'There!' said Gran, sounding triumphant as she flung open the door. 'This is your room.'

To my surprise, I did quite like it. There was a pleasing absence of frogs and the duvet was black and white. The whole room was black and white, no colours; it was smart compared to the rest of the house. 'I had it done up fresh when I heard you were coming,' said Gran. 'I asked around, found out what someone your age might like. I wanted lots of brightness, but everyone said, no, kids got more sophistication than that, she won't want lilac or pink or any of them sort of colours, so I said, OK, if you're certain.'

'It's nice,' I said. I didn't believe in overstatement the way Gran did. Nice was real praise. I sat on the bed and began to think better of Patience. She'd tried really hard to prepare for this visit. Then I felt guilty. I hadn't tried that much at all.

'The bathroom's next door,' said Patience, leading the way again. 'I like bright colours best, you know?'

I nodded as I looked round the orange bathroom with the yellow towels. The shower curtain had frogs on, and there was a frog-shaped soap with a thick layer of dust clinging to it. It had obviously never been used; there was an ordinary bar beside it.

I picked it up. 'You ought to get the dust off this.'

'If I wash it, the frog shape will disappear, fade before my eyes. I don't want that.'

'No, I guess not,' I said, feeling a little scared. Gran was crazy. I just hoped it wasn't hereditary.

'In the old days, this room used to be a little bedroom, so it's a good size.'

I nodded. Even when I'd stayed in a top New York hotel, the bathroom hadn't been as big as this. It was funny to find such a large smallest room in such a little house.

'Do you want to see my room?'

I nodded, though I didn't really; it seemed wrong, somehow, to go peering round your gran's bedroom, but on the other hand, I was curious.

Marley wandered in just ahead of us and installed himself *in* the bed, not on it. He snuggled down near the pillow and made himself completely comfortable. I decided there was no way he was getting into my bed like that, not ever. You could get all sorts of things; asthma, worms, fleas. It was disgusting.

'Is he allowed?' I asked.

'He's a law unto himself,' said Patience. 'I just let him get on with it.'

There were frogs in this room too. The print on the duvet cover was frogs, and there were matching frog curtains. It was obviously an obsession, this frog thing, and not a very healthy one. Gran needed therapy, I was sure of it.

'And now it's time for a nice cool drink and some cake.'

We went down to the kitchen where Patience got two cans of orangeade out of the fridge.

'Would you mind if I had tea?' I hated canned orange, it was sweet and sickly and it didn't quench your thirst.

'Tea?' asked Patience. 'I don't have it. I've never been one for all these English cups of tea.'

'I like coffee, I don't mind that instead.'

'I don't have coffee either, I prefer cold drinks, fruit juices and cans.'

I sighed. Whoever heard of a grown-up who didn't have tea or coffee in the house? It was ridiculous. Since there was no alternative, I took the orangeade. Gran drank hers straight from the can, but I asked where the glasses were. Without a glass, I tended to get hiccups. It tasted just as nasty as I'd expected, but at least it was ice-cold. Gran opened some biscuits which she began to eat, straight from the packet. I refused them; there was more than enough sugar in the drink.

After a while, I decided I needed to be by myself to think about everything that had happened. It had been such a full day, and Gran was pretty overwhelming. I made some excuse about wanting to unpack my things and went upstairs.

I hadn't shut my bedroom door, and Marley had found his way in. He was on my pillow, snoring. I grabbed him by the scruff of the neck and yanked him off. The bedding was covered in long black and grey hairs. I unzipped my bag and got out the radio, tuning in to the Classic station because it reminded me of Mum. I missed her already.

The *Neighbours* theme tune kept intruding from downstairs. Patience was obviously a fan of soaps. I'd spent three months in Australia the year before last and I'd watched it every now and then, but it hadn't impressed me much.

I felt restless, so after a while I wandered downstairs again, careful to shut the bedroom door first. Gran was stretched out on the sofa with her feet resting on the arms. The silver ankle boots had been kicked off and had landed halfway across the room. Gran was wearing bright-pink socks with teddy bears on them. She would, I thought.

Patience looked up and shifted her feet to make some room beside her, but I sat in the rocking chair opposite instead. '*Star Trek*'s on,' said Patience happily. 'It's a repeat of the Tribble episode. You remember them?'

I shook my head.

'You know, those fluffy things that multiply and fill the ship. A bit like furry balls. Cute. I kind of wanted one when I first saw it.'

I rolled my eyes, though I was careful that Gran didn't see me.

'I'll make some dinner after. What do you fancy?'

'I thought you only had bun and cheese.'

'I maybe have a few more things,' said Patience, and I knew that she'd fibbed about the lack of food in the house in the hope of eating chicken in a café.

'I don't know if I want anything.' My lack of appetite was genuine; I never could eat much when I was nervous, and everything was far too odd for me to be able to relax. There was nothing ordinary or normal about Patience. She wasn't the secure, comforting, sweet little old lady of my imagination, she was a half-crazy grown-up who kept pretending to be a child.

'You must eat, you know. When I was your age, I was eating three Shredded Wheat.' She laughed and then saw that I didn't get the joke. 'There used to be this ad on telly which said "Bet you can't eat three Shredded Wheat", but I guess you're too young to remember that.'

I just nodded.

'Have a little soup or something.'

I nodded again. Anything to keep Gran quiet.

'You won't mind if I have a proper meal? I'm famished,' Patience said.

We ate on trays in front of the television. It was quite homely, I thought, and I began to warm to Gran a little. But then I was forced to sit through some stupid cartoon video that was meant for four-year-olds. Patience thought it was the funniest thing she'd ever seen.

'You don't like it?' she said as it finished. 'I rented it as a treat.'

'It's a bit young.'

'I enjoyed it.'

'I rest my case.'

Gran nearly split her sides laughing. That was one

good thing about her; at least she didn't take offence.

In bed that night, I heard Gran laughing fit to bust over some late-night comedy. It was a grating sound when you were trying to get some sleep. I buried my head under the covers and tried to pretend I was in a nice, quiet hotel room. It was way past midnight before I fell asleep.

Four

I was up early next morning, but there was no sign of Gran; she was obviously still in bed. I showered and dressed and then wondered if it would be OK if I got myself some fruit juice and a slice of toast. I was hungry now, but it seemed wrong to begin breakfast in someone else's house without even asking. I sighed and went into the living room, making as much noise as possible in the hope that Gran would realize I was awake and get up herself. I realized then that I should have asked what time Gran usually woke up instead of just assuming it would be at a reasonable hour.

It was gone ten before Gran came down, her hair frizzing out all over the place and her lime-green dressing gown barely covering her ample figure. I looked pointedly at the frog clock on the wall but all Gran said was, 'Good morning, darling, sleep well?'

'Fine, thanks.'

'I always sleep like a log.'

'Yes,' I said. Then I remembered that Gran hadn't retired, she still had a job. 'Don't you have to go to work?' I asked.

'I mostly work from home these days. That's why

I've got the computer. I like it better this way. You can keep your own hours, stay in bed all morning if you want and work all night if the mood takes you.'

I didn't like this idea at all. I could imagine Patience clattering about at all hours when I was trying to sleep.

Patience must have read my expression because she said, 'Creative people work differently. I'd have thought living with Odette, you'd have been used to it.'

Mum always got fed up with people who used their so-called creativity as an excuse for a chaotic life. She was one of the most organized and disciplined people I knew. Maybe being dragged up by Gran had made her decide to be especially methodical. But I didn't say any of this to Patience, I just asked her if I could get myself something to eat.

'Haven't you had anything yet? How long have you been up?'

'Three hours.'

'And you haven't had breakfast?'

'I thought I should wait for you.'

Patience laughed and said, 'You are a strange one. You help yourself in this house. I don't have a sit down breakfast, there's no point with just one person, I have croissants or toast and such in my hand. But we could eat at the table now I suppose, if you really want to . . .'

'Yes, I'd like that,' I said. Mum and I had always made sure we had a proper breakfast together; it had been the high point of the day. I wanted to keep hold of my usual way of doing things. I didn't want to fall into the bottomless pit of chaos that my gran seemed to create around her.

Patience sighed. She obviously wasn't happy with the disruption to her normal routine either. 'Let me get dressed then,' she said. 'You could start to lay the table. The knives and forks are in the kitchen drawer. There's a tablecloth and some place mats in the dresser in the dining room.'

I was relieved that Gran had all the things you needed for a normal breakfast, even if she hardly ever bothered to use them. I found cereal and marmalade. There was also a toaster, so I made enough for both of us.

It took Patience ages to get ready. By the time she came down, the toast was cold. She didn't seem to mind though; she ate with great enthusiasm, smothering each slice in butter and marmalade. Watching her, I was surprised that she wasn't even fatter.

'What will you do today?' asked Patience.

'I don't know. What is there?'

'You've got a week before school starts. There's lots to do, I don't mind what you choose.'

'Yes, but what can I choose from?' I asked. I wasn't used to having so little direction. Mum was always very precise about what was required of me.

'Well, London has everything. Shops. Cinemas. Museums too, but they're boring, I don't want to do that.'

'You're coming as well?'

'There's lots of nice things we can do.'

'I thought I'd go somewhere by myself.'

'You don't know London very well. Besides, I'm not sure you're old enough.'

I sat back in my seat and looked at Patience. This was unexpected. Judging by what I'd already seen of her, I'd assumed there wouldn't be any rules about going round on my own. Patience obviously wasn't going to be consistent, which was going to be difficult. I liked to know where I was with people but my gran didn't fit into any category I could figure out. It was puzzling to say the least. 'I'd rather go on my own,' I said, wondering if Patience was open to persuasion.

'No. We'll go together. I want a nice day out.'

I almost replied that it wouldn't be a nice day out at all if I had to be seen with my gran. But it was clear that she wasn't going to budge, so all I said was, 'I think I'll stay here then, if you don't mind.'

'You don't want to go out with me?' asked Gran in hurt tones.

'It's not that . . .' I said, though we both knew it was. 'I'm still tired from yesterday.'

'We wouldn't have to be really energetic.'

I sighed.

'Tell you what, just come with me to the market. I have to buy a few things.'

'I'd rather stay . . .' I began, but then Gran's hurt expression started to get to me. 'All right then,' I said, 'let's go to the market.'

★

East Street was a bustling local market a short bus ride away from Gran's house. Stalls lined most of its length and they seemed to sell everything from shellfish to lampshades. I started to feel better as the liveliness of the place began to get through to me. There was reggae coming from one of the stalls, competing with a country singer being played at another. Every now and then, Patience bumped into someone she knew, quite literally; the street was so crowded that you couldn't help jostling everyone. Each person seemed delighted to see her. There was much hugging and shrieking with joy, followed by a barrage of questions about children and grandchildren and whether or not they'd got jobs yet or passed their exams. I was yanked forward and introduced to all with many exclamations about what a pretty child I was. By the time we'd got halfway down the street, I'd heard so much about my own charms and talents that I almost believed it. At least Gran seemed glad I was there. At least Gran seemed proud of me.

Far down the street, there was a man selling T-shirts, the kind I'd always dreamed of having. They were black with little specks of gold all over them and pretty scooped necklines. I picked one up and held it against myself.

'Lovely it is,' said Gran. 'I think you should have one. Here, I'll pay for it.'

'It's OK, I've got money,' I said.

'No, let me treat you, darling. I'd like that.'

I smiled, suddenly feeling full of goodwill towards

her. The man put my T-shirt in a wrinkled paper bag. Then Patience said, 'And I think I'll have one for myself. Lovely they are.' She picked up one four or five sizes larger and held it against herself. 'There,' she said. 'When we're wearing them, people will think that we're twins.'

I bowed my head, shamed even at the thought. 'I don't want it,' I said, pushing my own T-shirt back towards the stall holder.

Patience had her hurt expression again, with a touch of bewilderment thrown in. 'What's wrong?' she asked.

'What do you think's wrong?' I said through clenched teeth.

'Is it because I'm having one too?'

'We'll look silly,' I replied, too mortified to watch what I was saying.

'You think we'll look silly?' echoed Patience.

I didn't answer.

'OK, we'll just take the one,' said Gran to the stall holder. 'The small one. We'll leave the big one now.'

We walked away from the stall in silence. I'd never felt so mean. 'It's OK,' I said, 'go and get it, I don't mind really.'

But Patience didn't answer, so we just kept walking further down the street.

'I'm sorry,' I muttered, but there was no reply.

All through the journey back, I was aware that I had spoilt things. I remembered all the praise that had been bestowed on me when Patience had met her friends and how good it had been to feel wanted and admired. Now that feeling had gone. I clutched my T-shirt and wished I'd never set eyes on it. I'd been so happy to find it, but now I doubted that I'd ever want to wear it. I could be so stupid sometimes. I wished I hadn't come to London. I wished I was in Paris with my mum.

Five

Upstairs in my bedroom, I was listening to the sound of Gran's favourite reggae as it came up through the floorboards. I wondered how Patience ever got any work done, but she insisted that heavy rhythms helped her to concentrate. It was hard to see how.

I went into the bathroom to change. I wanted to look neat and cool, but not overdressed. I'd only been there five minutes when Patience started banging on the door. 'How long you going to be?' she said.

I was washing my face and hands. 'Only a few minutes,' I replied, but before I was even dry she was banging again. I opened the door crossly and let her in. I'd have to finish getting ready in my bedroom. Patience took up so much space. I don't just mean that she was large, she was sort of everywhere, all at once; she filled every room and I often felt unimportant beside her. I had as much right to be in there as she did. OK, it was her house, but I was living there too.

When I got to my bedroom, I found that Marley had sneaked into my bed. I slung him off immediately and he miaowed at me as if I'd half killed him. It certainly was tempting to commit an act of violence, but I restrained myself. I was actually in quite a good mood that day.

It was almost five o'clock and Beverly was due in half an hour, which was the main reason why I wanted to look my best. I was quite excited about seeing her again. I'd often wished for a brother or sister and, as a cousin, I thought Beverly might be almost as good. I wondered what Beverly would look like now. Would she be tall or short or fat or thin? We'd last met almost seven years ago. I tried to remember my impression of Bev. She'd been quite noisy, and rather skinny. But she'd been willing to share her sweets and toys and we'd played a really good game of Ludo, which I'd won. Patience had said we'd be going to the same school at the start of the spring term. I was relieved. It was hard being totally new, so it would be useful to have Beverly to show me everything and to help me to work out what to do.

Beverly was early, which was worrying. It seemed overeager and it was important to be cool. But she'd been brought by her father, Uncle James, so I decided she probably hadn't had much say in the matter.

James looked a bit like Mum, but he was well built and a lot taller. He put his arm around me and said, 'It's wonderful to see you looking so fit – I wish Beverly would stop looking like a wet rag. She doesn't eat enough vegetables.'

I took a good look at Beverly, who was twisting her hands in response to Uncle James's observations. I thought it was a bit mean of him to mention it, but he did have a point – wet rag was an apt description of Beverly's appearance. She was tall, but thin as she could be, and her eyes were big like satellite dishes. And she didn't stand in the hall calmly and sensibly, she kept jumping about as if she had some dread disease that kept you moving all the time in little jerks. But what was far worse than any of this was that she was wearing a faded blue quilted anorak, with white stitching that was coming unpicked, and a top that was at least two sizes too large for her, in a hideous shade of pink. Her legs were covered in a pair of tracksuit bottoms in murky grey but they stopped just above her ankles. She might have been a train-spotter. I couldn't help being aware of my own neatly hemmed jeans and cool white T-shirt. I tried to be gracious as I greeted Beverly, but inside I felt desperately disappointed. Beverly would show me up at least as much as Gran. She just wasn't cool, she didn't dress like any of the other black kids I knew. You've got to have style, it's the most important thing there is. If you don't look right, you're nothing, you're an embarrassment to your family and friends.

But Gran didn't notice how quiet I'd gone. She was all smiles; she even gave Beverly a hug. Uncle James complimented me some more and said he always listened to Odette when her recordings were featured on the radio.

'Take Bev upstairs, Grace, and show her your room. I'll be up later when I've had a chat with James. Then we'll play some games.'

Games? How old did Gran think we were? I looked at Beverly, expecting to see that she shared my horror, but she only smiled happily and said in a booming voice, 'That would be excellent, Patience.'

'Come on then,' I told her.

Beverly followed me upstairs and into the bedroom. I had been arranging it; my trunk had arrived mid-morning with all my favourite possessions: a CD system, my horror books, a camera, the grubby white dog I'd won throwing darts at a funfair when I was nine, and the photo album that had pictures of my mother in performance.

Beverly leaned against the bookcase and said how nice the room looked. This eased some of the apprehension I was feeling. But then she started mauling my things, picking up every book and ornament in sight, and passing some inane comment. 'This doll's so cute,' she said about a carved wooden figure done by a Native American that I'd been given in Canada. I frowned. It wasn't a doll and it certainly wasn't cute; it was a fierce looking bear on its hind legs.

'I used to stay in this room sometimes last year when my mum was ill in hospital and my dad was on the road,' said Beverly.

'On the road?'

'He drives a truck. He has to go to the other end of the country sometimes, or even abroad.'

I wasn't really very interested in the details of Beverly's life; I'd only asked because it had seem the polite thing to do. I put on some music to ease the tension. Beverly was still nervous. She could barely stand still; she kept hopping from one foot to the other and yakking about anything and everything. I couldn't see what on earth she was scared of. It was pathetic of her to be worried when she wasn't doing anything more than standing in her cousin's bedroom.

It bothered me to think that this room had once been Beverly's – or as good as. Perhaps, since she'd had it first, she had more claim on it than I did. To assert my right to it, I stretched out on the bed, without inviting Beverly to make herself more comfortable. I watched as she remained where she was, increasingly awkward. Picking up the remote control, I skipped the next track on the album. 'I hate that song, it's got such stupid lyrics,' I said.

'Yeah,' Beverly answered.

'Which track do you like best?' I asked her. It was a trick question. If Beverly was as dopey as she seemed, she wouldn't have any idea what was on the album.

Beverly mumbled something and I knew my guess was right; Beverly hadn't heard any of it before. There was no hope at all then; Beverly was a disaster. She came towards the bed, obviously hoping to be allowed to sit down, but I didn't make room for her so she was left hovering.

Uncle James came up to say goodbye. 'Stand still, Beverly, and don't stoop,' he said, smiling at me all the while. I felt a little sorry for Beverly then; he did seem rather critical. When he went, Gran returned and asked what we'd been up to.

'Just listening to some music,' I said with irritation. I was still full of disappointment that Beverly was so pathetic.

'And talking,' Beverly added in her loud voice, obviously anxious to please.

'Why don't you both come downstairs? I've just got Rampage.'

I had no idea what Rampage was, but Beverly actually clapped her hands in delight. It turned out to be a new computer game, and Gran and Beverly insisted on giving me a running commentary on how you played it. It was one of those blow-your-opponent-out-of-the-sky jobs, and I couldn't see any point in it whatsoever, but Patience and Beverly thought it was excellent beyond description.

They must have played that game for at least an hour and a half. Every now and then, one of them asked me if I wanted to take over, but each time, I refused. I had no idea how to play, and I wasn't going to look stupid learning.

So instead, I sat in the armchair and switched on the television.

Immediately, Patience said, 'Turn that down, Grace, we can't concentrate with that racket,' as if the bleeps and booms of Rampage weren't bothering me at all. For a moment, I just sat there, but then Patience shouted, 'I said, turn that down!' and I was startled into lowering the sound until it was barely audible.

You can watch sport without sound, and most cartoons, and soaps make much the same sense with or without the dialogue, but *Mastermind* is another matter. I sat watching Magnus Magnusson mouthing questions at the contestants and watched them mouthing back the answers without having the least idea what was going on. I could have changed channels, but it was most enjoyable to moan under my breath that *Mastermind* was educational, I could learn a lot from it, if only I could hear the sound.

Patience fired one last time, and the airship dropped without trace.

'Brilliant!' Beverly sighed.

'Tough luck,' said Patience. 'For a while, I thought you'd beaten me.'

Beverly shrugged happily. 'I've never beaten you, Patience, you know that.'

'You will,' Gran replied.

'You really think so?'

'You're not far off, and these rheumy old eyes are failing, and these fingers aren't as nimble as they used to be.'

Beverly started making this hideous honking sound that seemed to pass for laughter. I realized then that Patience had been joking; she didn't see herself as old at all.

'Time to eat,' said Patience, and we went into the kitchen. They ate heaped plates of sausage, egg and chips with tomato ketchup and ice cream to follow, but I picked at mine – Gran made me eat such junk – but skinny Beverly loved it. She cleaned her plate and then asked for more, causing Patience to grin at her in a pleased sort of way and say how lucky it was that one of her grandchildren had a good appetite.

Grandchildren. I rubbed my forehead, feeling foolish. Somehow, I'd managed to lose sight of the fact that Beverly was a grandchild too; as far as Patience was concerned, we were probably of equal importance. Or maybe Beverly counted more, because she'd stayed at the house ages before I had, and had lived just a few streets away for most of her life. Beverly and Gran weren't virtual strangers, they'd known each other almost for ever. That was evident from the game they'd been playing. They were easy with one another. They were practically best pals.

The thought made me uncomfortable, so I decided they were welcome to each other. What did I care whether I mattered to Patience or not? And as for Beverly, she was so grotesque that Gran was probably the only human being on Planet Earth who could stand to be anywhere near her.

The evening passed slowly. I went back up to my room. As I went upstairs, I made as much noise as possible, but I wasn't sure they even noticed that I'd gone. I tried to read one of my magazines, but it was hard to concentrate. Downstairs, Beverly and Patience were laughing hysterically, Gran's shrieks in perfect harmony with Beverly's honks. I felt bored and left out.

Almost an hour later, Beverly came upstairs to join me. 'Where did you get to?' she said, which I thought was a pretty stupid question.

'I felt like reading,' I answered, in case Beverly got the idea that I minded my exclusion.

'Patience is the best, isn't she? She's the only grown-up I know who really likes playing. I mean she doesn't pretend like most of them do, she enjoys it all as much as we do.'

Who's this *we*? I thought, giving Beverly a glare.

'You're so lucky to be living with her.'

'I know,' I said, my voice heavy with sarcasm.

Beverly evidently didn't understand irony because she looked really pleased with my response. 'She says why don't you come down? She says we can play something else if you can't do computer games.'

'I can do them,' I said hastily, 'it's just that they bore me stupid.'

'*Really?*' said Beverly, in much the same tone Gran had used, as if she could hardly believe it.

'Really,' I replied, mimicking the rather gruff pitch of Beverly's voice.

This time, Beverly knew she was being mocked, and she began her agitated hopping from one leg to another again.

It annoyed me. If Beverly was so pathetic that a bit of mild teasing was going to throw her into a panic, it was a wonder that she hadn't had at least three nervous breakdowns.

'Why don't you come back down?' said Beverly again, but her voice was kind, as if she knew that I was feeling sad and lonely.

This only made me madder. 'If I wanted to come

down, I would, OK? I don't need you or Patience to run after me.'

'OK,' said Beverly, but the way she looked at me gave the impression that for all her crassness, she knew just what was going on. I didn't like it one little bit.

Beverly didn't leave until gone nine. Patience called upstairs, 'I'm just going to take Beverly home, I'll be back in about fifteen minutes.'

'OK,' I called back.

'Bye,' Beverly shouted as she slammed the door. I hoped they'd notice that I didn't reply.

Six

I'd been to so many schools that I'd picked up a lot of experience along the way. And one thing I'd learnt was that you needed to get off to a good start. As soon as other kids saw you they marked you out either as someone who was worth knowing or as someone who wasn't.

Naturally, I always tried to fit into the worthwhile category. I've always been reasonably attractive and not stupid. I knew that in some schools, kids admired those who were good at sport, while at others, you had to be useless. I tried to weigh the situation up each time and give them exactly what they wanted.

Clothes counted, of course, especially if you were of African-Caribbean parentage – you had to have style, look the part. If you had to wear a uniform, you made sure your shoes were the latest fashion and that you carried your books in the right sort of bag. If there wasn't a uniform, you wore whatever the coolest kids your age were wearing. Hairstyles counted too; I always tried to judge the best look for African-Caribbean hair at any given time. And then there were things like having the right amount of money; too little and you looked poor, too much and you seemed to be flaunting it. And the other thing you needed was the right sort of relations. With Patience and Beverly, however well I did in other areas, I knew I was likely to make a very bad start indeed.

So on the first day of the spring term I studied myself apprehensively in the mirror, trying to work out the kind of first impression I would make. I decided that my hair was perfect, and the school sweatshirt looked clean and hung just right. The navy skirt I had to wear was precisely the right length, neither too long nor too short. My main worry was my shoes; although they were the latest from Miss Selfridge and had been shown in all the magazines, the soles were rather thick and the russet colour was one you either loved or hated.

'You ready, Grace?' called Patience.

'I'm coming,' I called back. I picked up my new bag and ran downstairs.

'We'll have to walk fast if we're going to be there on time,' said Patience.

'What do you mean, *we*?' I asked.

But Patience didn't respond, she was too busy putting her orange jacket over a purple shirt with matching purple trousers.

'I'm going by myself,' I told her firmly.

'Not on the first day,' said Gran. 'I have to take you to the head, she wants to talk to you.'

'I can find the head's office, that's not a problem.'

'They're expecting me to bring you.'

'They won't mind, honestly.' My tone was becoming increasingly desperate.

'I'm taking you,' said Gran, in a voice that suggested that she meant it.

'Please,' I said. I knew I was begging, but I couldn't stop myself.

'Come on,' said Gran, opening the front door.

I seriously considered making a run for it. I knew that Gran, size eighteen and none too fit, would never catch up with me. But somehow, I couldn't, so I trailed a little way behind, trying to pretend, at least to myself, that me and Patience weren't related.

Every now and then, Patience burst into song. She reserved this activity for the most public places: supermarkets, bus shelters and shoe shops. She had a slightly lower version for libraries, which she delivered not moving her lips, like a ventriloquist. This, she had explained, was because she'd been thrown out of a library once and she enjoyed borrowing books too much to risk it happening again.

'Couldn't you just not sing?' I'd asked.

Patience had shaken her head and looked as if I'd suggested that she should stop breathing. And here she was now, on the school route, singing full throttle, her rich, deep voice booming out a spiritual,and then the South African national anthem, followed by 'Lord of the Dance'. And just so that no one could possibly fail to notice her, she did little skipping movements as she went, in time to the music.

'Don't sing,' I said, through clenched teeth.

Patience ignored me, or perhaps she didn't hear.

'*Don't sing*,' I repeated.

Gran's voice trailed. 'Am I showing you up?' she asked with a little grin, but the singing stopped and it didn't resume again, not even when we went through the school gate.

Beverly came running to greet us. She was hopping again. Patience gave her a light hug and they began to chat about all kinds of nonsense, as if I wasn't even there. Whose first day is this? I thought morosely.

'I'll take you to the head's office,' said Beverly with great eagerness.

'We can manage,' I told her.

I'd seen Beverly three more times since the computer-games evening, and all my worst impressions had been confirmed. Beverly had not only continued to honk with laughter, but every now and then, she added a kind of braying to her repertoire. Her body twitched and jerked most of the time, sometimes almost imperceptibly, but at other times, it was all too visible. On this, the first day of term, she was behaving like a nervous wreck. I definitely didn't want to be seen with Beverly; her sweatshirt had frayed sleeves and she was shod in last year's trainers, bought off a market stall for a tenner.

But Beverly was slow to take the hint. She loped along beside me and Patience as we walked through the school corridors. I quickened my pace, but it was impossible to lose the dreaded relations; they stuck to me as if their existence was at stake. As they moved through the school, girls and boys turned their heads to stare at Gran, who was certainly a figure to be noticed. Then they looked at Beverly. A lot of the white kids stared at her with complete contempt. She seemed to confirm all the worst prejudices; she was gawky and stupid-looking and she had no pride. I cringed, but held my head high, willing them to look at me instead, which they did because my newness was unmistakable. I stared back, wanting to seem cool and unintimidated. I wanted respect. I wanted it more than anything.

Once we reached the head's office, Beverly had to remain outside. Patience rapped on the door. As we went inside, I saw that the head was a short, stout woman with permed hair and a dress made of crinkly yellow material with blue and red flowers printed on it. I decided that she and Gran would get on; they each had a passion for garish colours.

It turned out that they were old friends; Patience and Mrs Harcourt had practically grown up together. Listening to them wittering on about people they both knew and hadn't seen in ages, I felt a fool. Gran might have said she was a friend of the head, instead of just springing it on me like this. And what would people think if they knew? They'd probably assume I'd get special treatment or that I'd be in the head's office at all hours, spilling the beans about what the Year Sevens were up to.

'And you must be Grace,' said Mrs Harcourt at last.

I nodded and I think I probably looked pretty sullen. Then I realized this might not be the right response on your first day, so I changed my expression to one of sweetness and light and added, 'Yes, Mrs Harcourt,' with suitable meekness.

'I've put you in the same class as Beverly. I thought it would be nice for you to have a friend at hand, so to speak.'

'Yes,' I said, my tone forced. Just a few days ago, I would have been delighted, but a lot had changed since then. I knew it probably wasn't worth arguing about it, but I had nothing much to lose, so I added, 'I wouldn't mind being in a different class. I can manage on my own, it's fine.'

Mrs Harcourt looked at me with raised eyebrows, but all she said was, 'It's all been arranged. Beverly will take you to your home room shortly.'

Mrs Harcourt then forgot that I existed, and spent the next ten minutes asking after Gran's frog collection.

Then she went to the door and asked Beverly to come in. Bev bounced her way round the walls, obviously so excited about being in the head's office that she could hardly stand it.

Mrs Harcourt nodded at her and said, 'Will you take Grace to your home room now, dear?'

Beverly practically fell over herself and said, 'Yes, Mrs Harcourt,' before leading me outside.

In the corridor, I said, 'I'm not sitting next to you or anything like that.'

'I'm not in charge of seats, Mrs Power sorts that out.'

After that, we walked to the classroom in silence. Beverly opened the door, but I went in first. About twenty-five heads bobbed up expectantly and there was a brief hush.

'This is Grace Oswald,' said Mrs Power. 'Welcome to 7P, Grace. I'm sure that everyone will do their best to make you feel at home.'

'Are you Bev Oswald's sister then?' asked a tall girl who was sitting at the front.

'Don't call out, Carol Wilson.'

'Is she though, miss? They don't look like sisters.'

I was thankful for that at least, though suddenly I wished my mother had changed her name when she'd got married, the way that most people do. 'We're cousins,' I told everyone.

Beverly gave me her inane grin as if she was grateful to be acknowledged. Of course, she'd misunderstood completely; it was just that I preferred the class to know we were cousins than to think we were sisters and therefore even more closely related.

'I've put you next to Bev,' Mrs Power said. 'I'm sure she'll show you the ropes.'

'Yes, Mrs Power,' boomed Beverly. When she was sitting down and couldn't hop, she drummed her fingers on the table tops.

The morning passed slowly. There were so many new things for me to learn, not so much lessons, but the routines that every school had but which always varied in each new place. I found the work neither harder nor easier than usual but somewhere in between. Yet it was clear that Beverly struggled with everything. Her exercise books were a mess, all crossings out and smudgy rubber marks. She always added up using her fingers and muttering the numbers in a loud whisper. When she had to read in the English lesson, she stumbled over the words so much that the teacher got somebody else to do it. She was useless at science too; she spilt the contents of a phial and it splashed over the corner of my new textbook.

At dinner time, I managed to get away from her. I stood by myself in the concrete playground area and watched the other members of my class. The girls tended to wander round in pairs, exchanging secrets and telling each other jokes. The boys played more, kicking balls around or merely jostling with each other for the fun of it.

But there were three girls sitting on the steps together, looking at cards of some sort and talking and laughing with each other. I recognized one as Carol, the girl who'd asked if me and Bev were sisters. They were all of African-Caribbean parentage like me, and I'd noticed right from the start that they were the most important people in the class, the ones the others listened to. I walked up to them coolly, determined not to risk rebuff by seeming too eager. 'Hi,' I said. They raised their heads and gave me a slight nod, all in unison.

'What's your name again?' asked Carol.

'It's Grace,' I told her.

'I'm Merle,' said the pretty girl beside her.

'And I'm Jess,' added the other one. She was quite small with a thin little face and hair that was plaited and beaded.

'Which school did you go to before?' asked Carol. She was obviously the class inquisitor.

'It wasn't in this country, it was in California.'

This wasn't strictly true, the last school had been in Belgium, the one before had been the Californian one, but while there was kudos in spending nine months in LA, there was no gain from an education in Brussels. Suddenly, they looked interested.

'Beverly Hills?' asked Merle.

'San Francisco?' said Jess.

'I bet it was Hollywood,' said Merle.

'I bet she's lying,' said Carol.

'No, it's true,' I said, and I set out to prove it by giving them all the details I could think of about what it was like to go to school in America.

By the end of the afternoon, they were being quite friendly. I knew I wouldn't become one of them at once, it didn't happen like that, but they certainly weren't behaving as if they didn't want to know me and I was included in some of their jokes. At half-past three, Merle said, 'Where do you live?'

'Waring Road.'

'Well, if you want to walk home with Jess and me, you can, but whatever you do, don't let that Beverly come, she's rubbish.'

I shook my head; I had no intention of letting Beverly come anywhere near me once school finished.

'Do you and her get on?' asked Jess.

'No, we never have. In fact, I hardly even know

her. Apart from now, we were five when I last saw her. You can't help who your relatives are,' I added, thinking also of Patience.

'No it's true, you can't,' said Merle. 'I've got this boy cousin who likes country and western music.'

Howls of derision greeted this.

'And I've got a sister who wears ribbons,' added Jess.

'She is only five,' said Merle.

'Yeah, but still,' said Jess.

'Look out, there's Bev,' said Merle. and the three of us broke into a run, tearing down the road as though being chased by duppies.

After a few minutes, we stopped, breathless and giggling. 'Lost her,' said Merle. 'Praise be.'

'Praise be,' I repeated, but I felt uneasy just the same. I'd seen the look on Beverly's face as we'd started running. For the briefest moment, she'd had the lost look of someone who was frightened and hurting.

Seven

Once we reached the High Street, Merle said, 'I've got to get that sweatshirt I told you about. See you, Grace.' And she and Jess walked off into the shopping precinct.

I was disappointed. They might have included me in the buying. Maybe they didn't like me that much after all. Maybe they would have forgotten all about me by tomorrow. The thought nagged me all the way home and I became increasingly fed up. I remembered arriving at school that morning and having to walk along the corridors with Patience and Beverly. And I also remembered the shock of discovering that my gran thought it was all right to be friends with a head teacher.

As soon as I got home, I burst through the living-room door. I didn't even take off my jacket – all I could think of was the complete stupidity of my relations. 'Why didn't you tell me that you and the head are best buddies?' I asked Patience angrily.

She looked up from her word processing with a sigh. 'It didn't seem all that important. It won't affect you, will it?'

'Of course it will affect me,' I said impatiently.

'If the others find out, they'll think I've been planted like some sort of spy.'

'That's silly,' said Patience.

'No, it isn't. Anyway, what did you have to go and be her friend for? Heads don't have friends, it's a well-known fact.'

'It's not well known to me, and I'm sure Mary would be amazed to hear it; she's got more friends than anyone else I know.'

Gran was obviously making this up; heads lived in splendid isolation and this was all they deserved. I wondered if the rest of the class knew that Mrs Harcourt's first name was Mary. If not, I was bound to score a few points for being the first to find out. I wouldn't tell anyone how I'd discovered this though, and with any luck they'd never know that Mary and Patience were friends at all.

I leaned over Gran's shoulder. 'What are you doing?' I asked.

'I've got a deadline to meet.'

'What sort of deadline?'

'I have to answer these letters for the magazine.'

'Letters?'

Patience obviously didn't like being distracted from her work. She held up the magazine on her desk impatiently. 'See this?'

It was a copy of *Maribeth, the* teen mag. I bought it regularly – the stories were the best and it had pages of the latest styles.

'I sometimes answer the letters for the Dear Diana column. I do it freelance, they bring me in when the person who normally does it is on holiday or off sick or something. I've done the last four issues.'

'*You?*' The news was hard to take. I'd often pictured Diana as a beautiful young woman, full of concern for her fellow teenage sufferers. The idea that she was actually a grandmother who collected frogs was disappointing beyond description.

'It isn't true,' I said in a soft, sad voice.

'Believe me, today I wish it wasn't. I've got two eating disorders, four star-crossed lovers, three girls who are so desperate at home that they're thinking of running away and a child with a father who sounds like a maniac, all to be answered by five, and here you are distracting me utterly. For goodness' sake, go and watch TV or something.'

This was a side to Gran that I hadn't seen before. Up until now, she'd seemed glad of interruptions, seeing them as a welcome break, and she'd never been as cross as this, not ever.

As if reading my thoughts, Patience said, 'Sorry, Grace, I'm always a bit of a ratbag when I've got hard and fast deadlines to meet.'

'It's OK,' I answered. 'I'll go and do my homework.'

But up in my room, I didn't open my homework books. Instead I got out the last three issues of *Maribeth* and spread them out on the floor. I opened them on Diana's page, studying each letter and trying to hear Gran's voice in the replies.

It was strange though, Diana didn't sound like Gran at all; she sounded young and sensible and kind and concerned. Patience was obviously making it up, but why would she bother? Maybe it was some kind of joke. And yet, downstairs Patience hadn't sounded as if she was joking at all, quite the reverse, she'd sounded deadly serious almost for the first time since I'd known her.

I thought this over and decided that in fact I didn't know Patience at all. She was impossible to figure out, a really weird mixture of things. And I also felt cross with myself for not finding out before. I suppose I'd taken it for granted that Gran would be doing some boring elderly job that wasn't worth knowing about. I could have got free copies of the mag, most likely, and maybe other freebies besides. And they probably needed kids like me to do their consumer testing. I could have had anti-spot cream, with before and after pictures, and hair dyeing sessions. I could have modelled for them, perhaps. My imagination saw all kinds of potential advantages in being Patience's granddaughter.

It was hard to know what to think of my gran now. Reading the letters page, I realized that there was another side to her. Sometimes, she gave some quite good advice. And Diana never told any of the letter writers to stop whingeing and get on with it, she always tried to help instead. I pictured Patience downstairs being Diana and answering all those letters and thought how unpredictable life could be.

At half-past five, I went downstairs again. Patience was sprawled out on the sofa, watching television.

'Did you get it done?' I asked.

'Done and collected, ready to go to print,' said Patience. 'Now tell me what sort of day you've had.'

It had never been easy, talking to Gran; we didn't know each other well enough. But strangely, now I knew about the Diana page, I found it harder still. I think I was scared that everything I said would be seen as a problem that needed to be solved. And it was also hard to picture Gran, chaotic and not at all sensible, answering all those letters in such an organized, sensible way.

'How do you know what to say to the girls who write in to *Maribeth*?' I asked.

Gran grinned. 'It's mostly common sense. Some are serious problems, and then the advice you give is to tell someone, a teacher or even the family doctor. But then there's stuff like "my boyfriend's two-timing me". Well, we've all been there, haven't we? It's not hard to think of what to say.'

I hadn't been there. I'd never had a boyfriend. So far, I hadn't felt the need of one. I looked at Gran and tried to imagine anyone ever having the bottle to two-time her. I mean, you just wouldn't, I thought. It wasn't difficult to picture Gran in the old days, when she'd been twelve or thirteen; she probably hadn't looked all that different. Her face was lined but I was surprised to see that it wasn't really an old face, it was quite round, almost babyish, and full of smiles.

'When were you two-timed, Gran? – Sorry, I mean, Patience.'

And Gran began to tell me the story of her youth, with all its ups and downs, and explained about Grandad and how he'd been going out with another girl at the same time as he'd been dating her, but she'd made him choose and of course, he'd chosen her and they'd got engaged and later they'd been married.

'I miss your grandad,' said Gran, and she looked sad. 'He was full of fun, always laughing, always had something to say for himself. But he could listen too. These days, it's hard to get people to listen.'

I went over to the photo of my grandfather, Edgar Oswald. It stood on the sideboard next to a plant that had just come into flower. He looked a bit like Mum. He was tall and good-looking and he wore a suit.

'He was the first black man round here to be a school inspector. I was so proud.'

'Mum told me,' I said. 'I wish I'd got to know him better, but we hardly saw you at all because of all the moving around.'

Gran sniffed and I hoped she wasn't going to cry. Most grown-ups didn't, but with Patience you could never really be sure of anything.

Looking at Grandad's picture made me remember how much I was missing Mum. School hadn't been too bad, but it was early days yet; anything could happen. I'd much rather have been in . . . where was she at the moment? I glanced at the calendar on the wall but it was no use, it was last year's and was still turned to December.

'What's the date?' I asked.

'Search me,' said Gran. 'I think we're still in January.'

'I know that.' Sometimes, I wondered if Patience was senile. And then I remembered the Diana page and decided that Patience's marbles were mainly present and correct. My thoughts returned to Mum. From January 10th until the end of the month, she'd be in Madrid. If only I was there too, I thought, instead of here with Patience . . .

The phone rang. Gran picked it up and chatted in a pleased, excited way for the next ten minutes. It was Beverly. I could hear her voice bellowing through the phone. Eventually, Gran put the receiver down on the sideboard. 'She wants to talk to you,' she said.

'Tell her I'm out,' I mouthed, but Gran gave me such a dirty look that I picked up the phone without further argument.

As soon as Beverly began to speak, I had to hold the phone a foot away from my ear so as not to be deafened by it. 'What do we have to do for English homework?' she demanded.

We had to read a poem, even I knew that and I'd only been there a day. Then I remembered that Beverly knew too; I'd watched as she'd written down the information and put the collection of poems in her schoolbag. Suddenly I realized that this was just an excuse; Beverly was ringing to see if we were friends or not.

Not, I thought firmly, but I couldn't say so, not with Patience hovering by the phone.

So I pretended I hadn't seen Beverly taking all the details of the poem we were meant to learn, and I repeated the information for her, slowly and thoroughly, but with the minimum of words, so that Beverly would know that if she wanted proper conversation she'd have to whistle for it.

'Thanks,' said Beverly.

'Any time,' I replied, but my tone of voice said the opposite. I turned to Patience and asked if she wanted to speak to Bev again.

Gran took the receiver. 'I've been telling Grace about your grandad,' she said. And then, after a pause, she said, 'I know, Beverly, I miss him too.'

So Beverly missed Grandad. She would have known him then, known him properly, not just as some acquaintance, barely remembered, which was the way I saw him. Once again, I felt left out.

After the phone call, Gran went to make the tea. Sitting in front of the news, I thought about the family. It was funny to have a family you'd hardly seen. Beverly was close to lots of people: her mum, her dad and Gran. She even had a brother, whose name was Michael, but he was always busy, so I hadn't seen him again yet. I only really had Mum. Mostly, up until then, I'd thought it was enough.

Patience came in then and said, 'I thought we could listen to The Jammers when you've had your tea. I'm sure you'll love their new album.'

I knew their music already. It was raucous and off key and the rapper didn't sing, he shouted. Trust Gran to like them, trust her to have their latest album. I frowned my disapproval. I couldn't help wishing that my grandmother would start to act her age.

Eight

I'd been at Addison Hill Comprehensive for just over a week and so far, it had been better than I'd expected – unless, of course, I thought about Beverly.

Merle and Jess had been quite friendly. They had walked home from school with me each afternoon, and running away from Beverly had become part of our daily ritual. At first, I'd felt quite bad about this, but later I'd come to realize that if you were as gross and useless as Beverly, you were inviting people to be nasty to you, they really couldn't help themselves.

Jess and Merle stuck to each other though and sometimes I felt a bit left out. They'd known each other for so long that they had all sorts of secret sources of amusement that didn't make sense to anyone else. I often heard them giggling together and was irritated by it. It was rude to whisper and laugh in front of someone and not share the joke.

In class that morning, I looked across at Carol Wilson, who was easily the most attractive girl in the year, though sometimes she was pretty full of herself. She thought she was the wittiest person in the world, but sometimes she spoilt it by trying too hard to be funny. She knew a lot about music: ragga, rap and soul as well as classical. When I said that Odette Oswald, the soprano, was my mum, she'd actually been impressed, though the rest of the class had never heard of her and soap opera was the only kind of opera most of them knew. Still, it had been good to make Carol sit up and take notice; she was so cool and she was hardly ever fazed by anything.

Apart from Carol, Jess and Merle, no one interested me very much. They were easily the most important members of the class, the ones that everyone else had to listen to. I was glad that they seemed to like me; being shunned by them was a sign that you belonged in the zoo, and no one else bothered with you either. Beverly was definitely a zoo animal.

I caught Jess's eye and she signalled to me to be ready to receive a note. I watched as it worked its way round the class. As the rest opened it, they giggled and nudged one another. They were all looking in Beverly's direction, so it was obviously something about her. At last, I received the message. On the front, Jess had scrawled *EVERYBODY READ THIS EXCEPT BEVERLY.* I shielded it rather obviously with my arms so Beverly couldn't read it over my shoulder. It said, *Beverly stinks of dog do. Pass it on.* I giggled too. I hadn't noticed that Beverly smelt before, but once Jess had said it, it became obvious. Just my luck to be related to someone with a body odour problem.

I tossed the note surreptitiously to Carol. She grinned as she read it, but instead of ensuring that it escaped Beverly's notice, she placed it carefully in front of her.

Beverly blinked hard as she looked at the note and saw that she wasn't meant to read it. She hesitated for a moment, and then unfolded it. Watching her, I thought she was going to cry as she took in the words, but she merely lowered her head and screwed the message into a tight little ball that she shoved into her school bag.

The rest of the class was gazing at Beverly with interest. They were barely aware of Mrs Power's description of the original Globe Theatre. Who cared about what happened four hundred or more years ago when you could get such good drama in 7P's home room?

The bell went. I followed Jess and Merle outside. We sat on the wall, waiting to be allowed into the dining hall for lunch. 'Did you see her face?' said Jess, with a little squeal.

'I thought I'd die,' said Merle.

'Did you really have to let her see it?' I asked Carol. There was a slight tremor in my voice; I hated questioning her over anything, you could never be quite sure how she'd take it. And I didn't want her to stop liking me either. But for some reason, I needed to know.

She shrugged. 'She had it coming,' she said. 'Anyway, what are you so bothered about? What's she to you?'

'Nothing,' I said quickly.

Addison was the sort of school that provided

a balanced diet of fresh vegetables and salads at lunchtime – strictly no chips. Everyone complained about the pile of healthy looking veg they had to eat, but secretly, apart from carrots, I enjoyed it. I've always had sophisticated taste.

Beverly was sitting on her own at a small table by the wall. Every now and then, two or three kids would pass her, holding their noses. She pretended not to see them.

Merle nudged Jess and said, 'No one even speaks to her any more.'

I was suddenly overwhelmed with relief that I was smarter, better looking and more fun than Beverly.

Then two girls with long straight mousy hair went up to Beverly and said, 'You stink. All the black kids stink. You stink of dog do.'

Jess, Merle and Carol were deep in conversation and I don't think they heard it. I heard it though, and it made me uneasy. Jess had written that note, and she'd given some of the racist white kids all the ammunition they needed. I wanted to tell them off, make sure they knew that Beverly was one of us, but the truth was, she wasn't; we were ashamed of her. As I looked at her faded sweatshirt and market-stall trainers, I wanted to shake her, tell her she wasn't just letting herself down, she was letting us down too. Instead, I turned my head away. 'What's first lesson after lunch?' I asked Jess.

'Geography,' she replied, pulling a face.

I put on a similar look of disgust. Mr Exton, the geography teacher, was a vicious tyrant, aka Attila the Hun. I thought about the lesson with a happy sense of dread. There was something very comforting in going to the same school regularly; even the worst aspects were shared and therefore gave you a sense of belonging. Everybody hated Attila; you could spend ages recounting his most heinous crimes and shivering delightedly as you did so.

Only Beverly *really* seemed to dread the lesson; Attila hated her as much as the rest of the class did. He was always telling her off for producing smudged work. Her rubbing out produced holes in the paper. I'd told Patience what a mess she always made of things, and she'd said, 'Beverly's trouble is that she tries too hard, she does everything over and over and that's what causes all the rubbing out. She needs to calm down and not worry so much.'

I didn't see Beverly as a worrier – she was too brash to be the sensitive type in my opinion. Patience had adopted a caring, sharing role, which wasn't what I'd intended. I hadn't wanted to get sympathy for Beverly, quite the reverse. I wished I'd kept it to myself.

'Attila's the worst teacher in the school,' said Merle.

I gave a particularly good shudder to highlight the effect of Attila on my constitution. 'I know,' I said.

'He goes ballistic if you're late,' said Jess.

'I know,' I said again, repeating the shudder.

After lunch, me, Merle and Jess sat outside on the step. It was a cold winter's day, sunless and windy.

Every now and then, Jess blew on her hands to warm them. I shoved mine in my pockets. I wished I'd remembered to bring my woollen gloves.

Across the playground, Beverly was standing by herself against the wall. Every now and then, she looked towards me, as if expecting me to go over to her. I pretended not to see.

'I dare you to make Beverly late for the next lesson,' said Jess.

'No, I can't, Attila will go berserk.'

'You'll just have to make sure he thinks it's Beverly's own fault,' said Jess.

'How?'

Jess shrugged her shoulders. 'It's not my dare, it's yours. You have to work it out for yourself.'

'Yes, go on, I dare you to,' said Merle. She eyed me as if assessing whether I was worth being friends with or not.

'OK,' I said. It was the only possible reply.

For the rest of dinner time, I considered ways of delaying Beverly so she'd be late getting to the lesson. I supposed I'd have to take her aside, get her attention somehow, but then, unless I wanted a row myself, I'd have to ditch her somewhere.

Jess nudged me. 'It's nearly time for the bell. Don't forget, make her late.'

'Don't worry, it's all under control,' I replied.

But I didn't have a definite plan, so I knew I'd have to improvise. Feeling slightly nervous, I went over to Beverly and said, 'I want to talk to you. It's really important.'

Beverly looked pleased to have been singled out for my attention. 'I could meet you after school,' she said. 'We could walk home together.'

'No, I mean I've got a message for you.' Then inspiration struck. 'Mrs Harcourt wants to see you. It's urgent. She wants you to go up there now.'

Beverly looked suspicious. 'Why did she tell you? Why didn't she tell me herself?'

'She saw me, she couldn't find you. She knows we're cousins, she knew I'd pass on the message.' I could tell I wasn't sounding very convincing, but it was hard to find a more likely way of keeping Beverly back.

'And you're sure it's me she wants?'

'Double and quadruple sure,' I said. 'She told me. Why would I make it up?'

Beverly looked as if she could think of a dozen reasons, but then she said, 'It's not something at home is it? I mean, Mum isn't ill or anything?'

'I don't know what it is. I told you, Mrs Harcourt didn't say.'

'I bet it's Mum,' said Beverly. She began to run towards the school building just as the bell went.

Jess and Merle watched her go inside. 'What did you say to her?' Merle asked. 'She's running like Linford Christie.'

'Nothing much.' I was wishing that Beverly hadn't assumed there was something wrong with her mother. In fact, the whole idea was stupid altogether. Mrs Harcourt was bound to ask her why she'd come, she was bound to realize that someone must have sent her on a fool's errand.

I fell in with the rest of the class as they lined up outside the geography room. As I sat down, I was aware of the empty seat beside me that Beverly usually took.

Mr Exton began to give out Monday's geography homework. I'd only managed to score three out of ten; I'd never done much geography and Attila's approach was unfamiliar.

He paused by the empty space beside me and said, 'Where's Beverly Oswald?'

'I think she's gone to the toilet,' I told him, more because I wanted to protect myself than because I was concerned about Beverly.

'She had the whole of lunchtime,' said Mr Exton impatiently. He slapped her exercise book on her desk. As he walked back up the aisle, I took a look inside. Four out of ten. Beverly was getting better marks than I was and she was thick as anything.

Mr Exton began to speak in his usual droning voice about nothing much. I switched off and watched the classroom door. Beverly would come in any minute. Would she have told Mrs Harcourt who had sent her? Would Mrs Harcourt come herself and dish out punishment? What would it be? Detention? A letter home? Exclusion?

The classroom door opened. Beverly came in. She'd been crying, I could tell. Merle nudged Jess and they looked up too, waiting for the showdown with Exton. Beverly handed him a piece of paper –

obviously some sort of note. Her nose was running. She sniffed. I wished she'd use a handkerchief. Exton read the note in silence, and then, still without speaking, motioned her to be seated. She slipped into the space beside me. Nothing more was said.

I looked at the picture in front of me of a disused coal mine. What an anticlimax. No row, no shouting and strutting from Attila. No impressed Merle and Jess. They probably thought I'd messed it up. And somehow I had – at any rate, it certainly hadn't gone as planned. I knew I'd probably get a summons from Mrs Harcourt soon. And Gran would hear about it too – she was bound to, they were friends.

I worried all that afternoon. When school finished, Merle and Jess gestured to me to walk home with them as usual, but I shook my head and went to find Beverly.

She was still putting books into her bag in the home room. As I came back in, she looked up, then down again quickly, her shoulders hunched.

I said, 'What happened then?' as casually as I could.

Beverly didn't answer. Instead she said, 'Why did you pretend my mum was ill?'

'I didn't. You just assumed.'

'And you let me go on assuming. You let me think something was really wrong.'

'It was just a joke, that's all.'

'Funny kind of joke!'

'Look, I'm sorry, OK? I thought you'd see the funny side of it.'

Beverly brushed aside the one tear that slid down her face. 'Mrs Harcourt said whoever did it was very spiteful and mean. She gave me a note for Mr Exton so I wouldn't get into trouble for it. She said if I found out who it was who'd given me the wrong message, I was to tell her at once.'

I looked at Beverly in surprise. 'You mean you didn't tell her it was me?'

Beverly shook her head. 'I told her I didn't know the girl's name.'

'Why didn't you tell her?'

'I don't know,' said Beverly, but I was sure she had some secret reason. She picked up her bag and walked through the door without looking back. I followed slowly. I didn't understand.

Nine

Jess and Merle were still waiting for me as I came out of school. It was a pleasant surprise. I'd been scared that we wouldn't even be talking any more because I'd messed up the dare. 'I'm sorry she didn't get into trouble,' I said. 'I did try.'

'Can't be helped, I suppose,' said Jess. 'Exton's unpredictable these days.'

'Tell us how you made her late,' said Merle.

I explained with lots of gaps and pauses. Everything I'd done sounded pathetic now.

Jess said, 'You should have worked out that it would get you into more trouble than her.'

'I know. It's like I said, I did try, it was just that you didn't give me a lot of time.'

'It wasn't our fault,' said Jess hotly.

'No, I know it wasn't.'

'Why did you want to speak to Beverly just now?'

'I had to find out if she'd told Mrs Harcourt that I sent her up there.'

'Had she?'

'No.'

'Why not?' asked Merle.

'I don't know. I haven't figured it out.'

'I reckon she's hoping to blackmail you,' said Jess.

There was a small patch of waste ground not far from the school, and opposite, there was a sweet shop. 'Got any money?' Jess asked me.

'A bit.'

'I'm skint. I wouldn't mind a Mars or something. Merle wouldn't say no, either, would you?'

Merle giggled. 'Ever known me say no to chocolate?' She put her left foot on the low wall. 'What do you think of my shoes? They're new, I only got them last week, for the start of term. I almost got ones like Grace's, but I prefer these.'

'I saw yours,' was all I said. I was glad really, that we'd got different pairs, because I'd have hated it if we'd ended up looking like stupid twins, but at the same time, I was worried because Merle had rejected mine. Perhaps I'd bought the inferior ones.

'Are you going to get the chocolate then?' asked Jess.

I nodded and went in the shop while the others waited outside.

I returned with three Mars bars. Jess ate hers as if she hadn't eaten all day. 'School dinner was disgusting,' she said, by way of explanation.

'All that rabbit food,' I said.

'It's good for you,' said Merle. 'I like salad. That's why I have such a good figure.'

'You reckon?' said Jess. 'I'm skinnier than you any day of the week.'

'But not as skinny as Beverly. She's anorexic, she's got to be.'

I thought of the vast amount that Beverly had

eaten on each of the occasions she'd come to visit. 'I don't think she is, I think it's nervous energy.'

'My mum has that,' said Merle. 'She says it comes from running your own business. You worry all the time about VAT and profit margins.'

'Do you?' I said. Merle was always able to impress me. She knew such a lot about life.

'Did you know my mum and dad have invented this special Caribbean sauce? All the major supermarkets are going to carry it. It's called Selina's Sauce, after Mum. We're almost rich. We don't even bother with the lottery any more.'

'We didn't get a single number three weeks running. My dad thinks we should pack it in,' said Jess.

'You pack it in and that's when your numbers come up,' said Merle. 'It's obvious.'

We began walking again. Jess's Mars was gone, but Merle was still licking the chocolate off hers. I preferred to take very small nibbles.

'Beverly has free school dinners,' said Merle.

'Do you have them?' Jess asked, looking at me.

'No, I don't,' I answered, using the visible shudder technique to prove the point.

'I thought you did when it was in the family.'

'We're only cousins, and we're a lot of times removed.'

'What's removed?' asked Jess.

'It means you're more distant,' said Merle.

'A million miles apart,' I lied.

'Show us where you live then,' demanded Jess.

I had this image of Patience standing at the front

gate, arms outstretched to greet us. 'Another time,' I said. 'Show me your place, Jess.'

'I asked first.'

'Come to mine,' said Merle. 'It's on the way. Mum's getting in chocolate brownies this evening, as a treat.'

'Thought you didn't like junk food,' said Jess.

'She only gets the ones with the best ingredients. We wouldn't have rubbish,' Merle replied.

Merle's place was only round the corner from Patience's house, but it might have been on the other side of the world. The houses in her road were all large and detached and they had drives with rhododendron bushes. My wish to be counted as one of Merle's friends increased.

'We only moved here last year, when it looked like Selina's Sauce was taking off. It still needs a lot doing to it.'

There was scaffolding up one wall and a man was daubing something on the brickwork.

Jess walked up and examined his work. 'Not good,' she said, as she rejoined us. 'You should have got my brother in, I told you he'd do a great job.'

Merle shrugged. 'Nothing to do with me. You know what parents are like. They just won't take advice.'

I knew this all too well. If Mum had listened, I'd have been in Rome by now, in all that warmth and sunshine.

Merle let us in through the back door. 'I'm home, Mum,' she shouted. There was no reply. 'Still at work,' said Merle. 'Good. We can play the music really loud.'

Merle went into the room adjoining the kitchen and turned some music on. Jess started to dance but then seemed to think that no one was bothering to watch and stopped. I followed Merle towards the fridge. The brownies had already been piled on to a large plate. 'Help yourselves,' Merle said. We sat at a round wooden table. The vibrations from the speakers could be felt through the floorboards.

'Isn't it a bit loud?' I asked.

'No neighbours,' said Merle. 'That's the beauty of detached property.'

'You're so lucky,' said Jess. 'Our neighbours bang on the wall if you so much as breathe.'

'You can't make much noise in hotels either,' I said, not to be outdone, but my comment went unnoticed. Jess was busy helping herself to another brownie and Merle was pouring herself a glass of Diet Coke. It always seemed like bragging to go on about all the travelling I'd done, uninvited, so I had another brownie too, though I picked out all the nuts. 'What make are these?' I asked.

Merle held up the packet. 'You have to defrost them,' she said.

I nodded. Patience would love them. Maybe I'd try to get her some one of these days.

Jess opened the fridge door and took out a sausage roll. 'You don't mind, do you?' she asked Merle.

'I do, actually,' Merle said. 'You should ask *before* you help yourself, not after.'

Jess shrugged and replaced it.

'I didn't say you couldn't have it,' said Merle.

Jess got it out again and put some of Selina's Sauce on it. 'Who was that woman who brought you into school on your first day?' she asked me. 'Only she seemed a bit weird. I think I've seen her with Beverly too.'

'Oh, just someone I know.'

'Her coat was orange.'

'Was it?' I said.

'You must have noticed.'

'*Everybody* must have noticed,' laughed Merle.

Luckily, before I could be placed in the awkward position of having to disown Patience even more, Merle's parents came home. Me and Jess left shortly after.

'Have you and Merle been friends for long?' I asked her.

'Since Reception class. She's OK but she's started to think too much of herself since Selina's Sauce. She never stops talking about it. I've been thinking she might not be such a good friend to have. You have to watch her too. She doesn't always tell the truth.'

'How do you mean?'

'It's not for me to say. You just have to watch her, that's all.'

I slowed my pace. Jess was shorter than me and she was dawdling too, so we weren't covering a lot of ground. I thought it was good news that Jess and Merle weren't as thick with each other as they'd seemed and decided there might be room for me after all. 'What about Carol?' I asked.

'What about her?'

'Is she OK? Do you like her?'

'She's a laugh,' said Jess. 'She does all these things to kids, even to teachers sometimes, just for a laugh.'

'To teachers?'

'Yeah. She put superglue on Mrs Leeson's desk when we were in the juniors. She nearly got excluded, her books lost all their covers and it took hours to clean the desk. They would have made Carol do it, only they were worried her skin would stick or something.'

'Why didn't they exclude her?'

'She's really clever, the cleverest kid in the school, probably. Her parents got in this psychologist and he said Carol did things because she was bored – the school didn't stretch her enough.'

'She doesn't seem clever.'

'She only bothers when she feels like it. She'd rather muck about.'

'But do you like her?' I repeated.

'I wouldn't get on the wrong side of her, I'll tell you that much.'

'Why not? What would she do?'

'It's not for me to say,' Jess answered. Then, after a brief pause, she added, 'I saw her crush a person's hand once.'

'Whose?'

'It was Beverly's. She stamped on it when she fell over. She nearly broke her fingers.'

'Why?'
'Who knows?'
But I still liked Carol. She was always so cool.
'She hates your cousin even more than we do.'
'Why?'
'She's like that. She takes dislikes to people sometimes. In the juniors it was someone called Liz Deacon. I don't know why. I turn off here. Can I come to your place some time then?'
'Sure,' I said. 'I would have had you round today, but I have to ask my gran first.'
'Is she the woman who brought you to school that time?'
Jess was persistent. It was worrying. But before I could answer, she stepped off the pavement without looking where she was going. A car screeched to a halt. The driver swore. And Jess's question was forgotten.
'Take it easy, man,' she called out to him.
'You stupid black idiot. Why don't you look where you're going?'
'Why don't you learn to drive?'
The man shouted something very rude and sped off. I was still shaking, but Jess seemed perfectly calm. She continued to stroll across the road, waving goodbye as she reached the other side. Then she broke into a run. I watched until she was out of sight. Jess was OK. She was fun to be with. She wasn't scared of anything. I thought she'd be a useful friend.

Ten

Beverly seemed to have accepted that we could not be friends. She no longer gave me wistful looks, nor did she hover around after school in the hope that we might walk home together. She kept herself separate from everyone, or rather, everyone kept away from her.

Then Patience announced that she was to be one of the speakers at a conference on adolescent behaviour and I was required to stay with Beverly.

I looked at Patience in horror. 'I can't!' I said.

'Why on earth not?' asked Gran.

'Because . . .' I didn't know how to explain.

'Don't you and Beverly get on?'

'That's an understatement.'

'I wouldn't have expected you to be so childish, Grace.'

Coming from the grandmother who thought orange was the best colour in the universe, who loved eating puddings in American diners and who played computer games when she should have been working, that was pretty rich. I just stared.

Then she delivered an even worse insult. 'I would have thought you and Beverly would have got on like a house on fire,' she said. 'You're two of a kind.'

'*What?*'

'You're very similar.'

'No we're not. How could we be similar?'

'If you don't know, I'm not going to tell you.'

'You're not telling because you don't know either.'

Patience gave this chuckle. 'You're so funny when you're cross,' she said.

I felt the blood rush to my face. Here I was, upset, angry, *suffering*, and my grandmother was laughing her head off. 'Stop laughing at me,' I said.

'Don't get yourself into such a state, Grace, and then I won't need to laugh about it, will I?' Patience stood there, her shoulders shaking and her fat belly wobbling.

'I hate you!' I said, no longer able to contain my fury. 'You're stupid and fat and old!'

Gran said nothing, but she stopped laughing and her body stiffened. I knew at once that I had hurt her badly. 'Go on, get out of my sight,' said Patience eventually. 'Come back when you're in a better mood.'

And that was all. I slunk up to my room, beads of sweat forming on my nose and forehead. I sat very still for a long time, thinking over what had happened. How could I have said those things to my grandmother? What if she told Mum? She'd never forgive me. She always said respect for elders was one of the most important things in the universe. Back in Jamaica, kids were brought up to be good to their parents and grandparents. You never cheeked them like that. Mum called Jamaica home, even though she'd been born in London. She said we had to keep home values or we'd lose our sense of who we were and everything would come apart.

I stayed on my bed, still feeling scared, and listened. The house was totally quiet. Patience wasn't playing music or singing or clattering about with pots and pans. I'd never known it to be so silent.

I thought over the last few days. I liked Merle, Jess and Carol, but sometimes I wished they wouldn't get at Beverly so much. It was making life difficult; Bev could easily tell her mum and dad or Patience and where would I be then? I wondered what it would be like at Beverly's house while Patience was away. I hadn't been able to visit before because Beverly's mum hadn't been well enough. How long had Patience said she'd be gone? Two whole days and a night. A long time. It was funny to think of Gran giving speeches and being listened to. She didn't seem to be the sort of person you could take that seriously.

The day of the conference was wet and cold. I put on my long, hooded jacket with the quilted lining and waited for Gran to finish checking that she had all the notes she needed for the talk she was giving. She was getting agitated. 'I can't find anything,' she kept saying. 'Come help me look.'

I did help once or twice, but it was a thankless task. 'No, not there, I've already looked there,' said

Patience, wherever I went, so in the end, I wandered outside and sat on the wall.

The street was short but it was lined on either side with small rowan trees that were just starting to bud. I quite liked British seasons; everything was always changing. Once more, I thought about touring with Mum. We used to be in a different city every few weeks, with a whole new, exciting set of things to see. I'd written to her the previous day. I'd wanted to say that I hated London and wished she'd come and take me back with her, but at the last minute, I'd changed my mind and scribbled the usual note about being OK and making friends at school. It wasn't that I had any wish to remain with Patience, it was more that I didn't want to disappoint Mum. She was expecting me to behave in an adult way, to enjoy being with the other members of the family, and I didn't want to let her down.

That weekend, I would be with the family with a vengeance. I was dreading it. If only Beverly had been like Merle or Carol or Jess. But she was such a mess, always so silly and boring.

Patience came out at last and we set off for Beverly's house. It was only ten minutes' walk away and I decided that if I really couldn't stand being there, I could easily go back home until Gran returned.

Beverly's house was just like Gran's to look at. It was a grey-brick terrace which had a bay window in the front and a very short path leading to the door. Patience knocked and Beverly came down, closely followed by her older brother, Michael.

I couldn't remember when I'd last seen him. He was seventeen and went to college, where he was doing a catering course. Beverly had boasted that he could cook anything, even the most complicated meals, but I had barely listened. Nothing Bev had to say could ever be worth hearing.

'I'm late,' said Patience, bouncing up and down and doing an impression of the white rabbit.

'It's cool,' said Michael. 'I'll run you to the station on the bike.'

Patience beamed. 'You sure?' she said.

'Sure I'm sure,' said Michael. He picked up Patience's bag and carried it over to the gleaming black motorbike that leaned against the kerb. He put it in the large metal carrier on the back. Then he produced two crash helmets – I didn't see where they could have come from, it was as if he had magicked them. Gran strapped hers under her chin. She looked like some blobby alien. Then she climbed on the back of the bike and grabbed hold of Michael's waist. He kick-started the machine and they swept down the street. Uncle James appeared on the step just as they began to fade from view. 'You be careful, Michael, she's not so young . . .' he began, but his words were lost in the roar of the machine.

I just stared. I was impressed in spite of myself. I knew I'd never get on the back of a bike, I'd be too scared, but Patience had been fearless.

'I love Mikey's bike,' said Beverly. 'He once let me ride pillion. We were in this field, so it was absolutely safe. Dad was there too.'

I turned to Uncle James for confirmation. It seemed so unlikely that Beverly could enjoy something I was scared of. He nodded and said, 'Just like a boy,' with a sad sigh.

Beverly took his hand and said, 'You're so old-fashioned, Dad,' as they went indoors.

The house was bigger inside than Gran's and the decor was tamer – no frogs, for one thing. There was a large piano in the living room that took up half the floor space. 'Your mum and I used to have singing lessons. We also learned to play the piano on that,' said James. 'I preferred television. Looks like Odette wasn't as daft as she seemed.'

I smiled back at him; I knew that Mum was seen as the success in the family.

'Come upstairs and meet my mum,' said Beverly.

It was funny how much quieter Beverly seemed when she was in her own house. She moved normally, she didn't bang about, and she spoke in an ordinary voice; she didn't honk or boom.

Patience had told me that Beverly's mum had been ill with a virus for a long time. She was getting better, but it was happening slowly. I was a bit nervous of meeting someone who was ill and as I went upstairs with Beverly I wished it was possible to refuse. But Auntie Donna was sitting up in bed, listening to a tape of a book about South Africa and she smiled and talked just like anyone ordinary.

'I'm so glad to see you, Grace, it's been so long. Has Bev been looking after you?'

I mumbled something and felt embarrassed.

'I really wanted to come and say hello the day you arrived. Do you like living here in London? I expect you miss your mum.'

I was relieved that Auntie Donna had decided to answer that particular question herself. I couldn't really say that I didn't like living in London with Gran, it would have been rude. Ever since I'd told Patience that she was fat and old, there had been a change between us. Patience had stopped being so friendly. She was calm, and polite enough, but she was much cooler towards me than she'd been before, and the fun had gone out of things. She hardly laughed now, and she didn't sing when I was around. I hadn't imagined that I would ever miss my gran's exuberance, but now I wished there could be a return to all the silliness that had embarrassed me so much before.

As we left her mother's room, Beverly said, 'What do you want to do now then?'

'Dunno.'

'Well, do you want to watch television?'

'What else is there?'

'We could go for a walk, or round the shops.'

Normally, I would have said yes straight away. I needed a new pair of trainers – I'd found a hole in mine the day before – but I hadn't had an opportunity to get them. But there was no chance that I was going to be seen out on the street with Beverly, who'd be wearing that awful blue anorak and show me up totally. 'Let's stay here,' I said firmly. 'I think there's quite a good film this afternoon.'

The film was one that I'd seen at least five times before. I sat in front of the television, feeling bored and fed up. Why had Patience gone off like that? Didn't she know you were meant to cherish and protect your grandchild? You weren't supposed to expose her to the dangers of being bored to death by dull, inferior relations.

Michael came home. He said Patience had caught the train with seconds to spare.

'Can Grace sit on your motorbike?' asked Beverly.

Michael looked as if he was going to refuse, but then he said, 'OK.'

'It's all right,' I told him hastily. I didn't want to be anywhere near it.

'Oh, go on,' said Beverly. 'You'll really like it.'

'I said no.'

Michael gave me a look which suggested that I ought to be more polite to his sister. I was embarrassed again. He was nice, Mikey, he wore the best clothes and he had a smooth, cool voice with a slightly American accent. 'OK, I'll sit on it,' I said.

'Don't trouble yourself,' said Mikey, and he walked out of the room.

Mikey's obvious disapproval was hard to take; I really wanted him to like me. I sat on the faded sofa with my feet tucked under me and looked after him wistfully. Maybe I shouldn't have been so mean to Bev in his presence.

Beverly was watching me curiously, so to put her off the scent I said, 'Your brother really thinks he's a big man, doesn't he?'

'He's a lot bigger than you are.'

'In centimetres, maybe, but nothing else. Isn't there anything to do in this house except watch television?'

'No,' said Beverly.

I decided that Bev was deliberately being as unhelpful as possible. 'You mean that's what you do all the time, just watch TV?'

Beverly shrugged. 'I like television,' was all she said.

'Where's my room? I think I'll go up and read a magazine.'

'We're sharing,' answered Beverly.

For a moment, I was speechless. Then I said, 'I'd rather have a room of my own.'

'Well you can't. We don't have the space. Do you still want to go up there?'

I didn't. I'd wanted somewhere private, where there was no danger of Beverly intruding, but I knew that if I went up to her room, she'd probably come too.

She opened a cupboard and pulled out a few video tapes. I'd seen all but one of them before. 'What's this about?' I asked, picking it up.

'Patience bought it for me. We saw it together at this giant multiplex that had ten screens and I liked it so much that when it came out on video, she gave it to me for my birthday.' Beverly was booming again, and hopping too. 'It's about a family in the wild west, and when their parents die, they have to travel across the country to find an uncle who'll take care of them.'

The plot sounded all too familiar to me. Still, beggars couldn't be choosers, so I told Beverly to put it on.

We spent most of the afternoon in front of the television screen – or at least, I did. Beverly kept going upstairs to see how her mother was and fussing around with cups of tea for her. She vacuumed the house too and washed the kitchen floor. I knew I should offer to help, but I'd never had to do any cleaning before. Other people did it for you when you lived in hotels, and when we stayed in our flat in Paris, we had a daily cleaner. I didn't know one end of a broom from the other, and I didn't want Beverly to realize this. Beverly might laugh or call me stuck up. She'd probably tell everyone. It was so embarrassing, the stuff I didn't know. That was one of the hardest parts about growing up on the move with a famous mother. There were all kinds of things that never got explained to you. As Beverly dusted, I almost envied her. She knew how to do ordinary things. And she was a member of a proper family, with a mother, a father and a brother.

Mikey came back for a while and asked Beverly if she wanted a bar of chocolate. When she said she did, he went out quickly to the corner shop and brought one back for me too. I thanked him as nicely as possible and tried to be polite to Beverly while he was around. It wasn't easy though. And there was a night and another whole day to get through yet.

Eleven

Beverly's room was so small that once the spare bed had been put in there, you had to climb over it in order to get to the door.

'I can't sleep in here,' I said. I was almost in tears.

All Beverly said was, 'You have to, I'd told you, there isn't anywhere else.'

If I could have run out of the room without an undignified scramble over the mattress, I would have done so. Instead, I turned my head away so that Beverly wouldn't know that the tears were real and not just put on for effect. I felt so cramped in that little room. It was bad enough sleeping so close to someone when you were best buddies, but when you hated their guts it was totally impossible.

Beverly felt awkward about it too, I could tell from the way she undressed. As she got into her pyjamas, she kept up this running commentary on every action she made. 'My left leg won't go in these pyjama bottoms, my foot keeps getting stuck.' And then: 'The button holes are too big and the buttons keep coming undone.'

I wondered why Beverly thought I cared about her pyjama trousers and buttons. I was far too busy trying to get into my own pyjamas to worry about anyone else's. 'It's because there's so little space,' I said, half to myself. Then I added, 'You should get a bigger house.'

'This is the biggest we could get on the money my mum and dad earn,' said Beverly.

She must have been thinking it was stupid of me to imagine they'd stay in such a small place if they could afford anything larger. I wished I hadn't said it and was embarrassed into silence. Even in the half-light, I could see that Beverly was upset. It wasn't that I meant to be nasty to her – well, perhaps I did mean to, in a way. Otherwise, Bev might think we could be friends in school time. And then Merle and Jess would stop including me in things. And, most worrying of all, they might decide that I deserved to be made fun of and despised as well. I knew that as long as everyone was busy hating Beverly, they wouldn't have any time left for hating me.

Years ago, when I was very young, I'd gone to this school where I hadn't fitted in at all. I don't know why. Perhaps it was because I'd been small for my age then (though I'd grown to normal height since). Or maybe it was because I'd been one of the few black kids in a mainly white school. Whatever the reason, although it had only happened to me once, I still remembered it. I even had nightmares about it. The other kids had teased me every day; they'd thrown away my books and scribbled on my work and done their best to make my life miserable.

I'd learned then that if you wanted to be treated OK, you always had to make sure they picked on someone else.

Beverly got into bed. 'Shall I turn the light out?' she asked, stretching towards the lamp that was clipped to her headboard.

'I haven't finished undressing yet.'

Beverly sighed deeply. 'I thought you were ready. You seemed ready a minute ago.'

'I'm going to put on my long-sleeved pyjamas. This room's cold.'

Beverly ignored the criticism of her room and said, 'You mean you brought two pairs, just for one night?'

I cast a look in her direction that suggested a mixture of pity and contempt. Then I remembered that the light wasn't strong enough for Beverly to see, so instead, I said, 'Of course. Wouldn't you?' in a tone which implied that Beverly was the strange one.

Beverly said, 'It's funny, sharing this room. I've never had to share it before.'

I just grunted. I was thinking that Beverly probably snored.

'Are you ready now?'

'OK, turn the light out,' I said.

There was a short silence while we each adjusted to the darkness. Then Beverly said, 'You know that time you sent me to Mrs Harcourt?'

I wondered if it was worth pretending to be asleep. I wasn't going to answer, anyway.

'Well, I never told her. I said I wouldn't, and I didn't.'

I turned over. What did she want, a medal? It had just been a stupid trick, nothing more, it didn't need all the fuss that Beverly was giving it.

Still, as I thought about it, in Beverly's room, in the dark, I began to feel guilty again in spite of myself. Maybe it had been OK of Beverly not to tell. Maybe I did owe her one for that.

'You know,' Beverly went on, 'you shouldn't hang around that Carol so much. She used to beat up the Reception kids when we were in the juniors.'

The brief, good feeling that I'd had towards Beverly disappeared. Who did she think she was, trying to dictate which people I should go around with? What business was it of hers? But instead of taking the hint from my steely silence, Beverly continued, 'Carol trod on my hand once. Deliberately. I could hardly write for a week.'

This was the incident I'd heard about from Jess, but I didn't let on I knew, I just said, 'I expect you asked for it.'

'I didn't. I didn't do anything.'

At that moment, as far as I was concerned, Beverly asked for it just by breathing. 'Anyway, you're so hopeless at written work, I shouldn't think it made any difference,' I told her.

'It did,' shouted Beverly.

'Be quiet, you'll wake the whole house.'

'Don't tell me to be quiet in my own house,' returned Beverly. 'You're the visitor, not me.'

'I'm the guest. You should make me feel welcome. You shouldn't tell me who I can be friends with and who I can't.'

There was another pause and then Beverly said, with her usual boom, 'Sorry.'

I stiffened with irritation. For a moment, I'd thought Beverly might be going to stand up for herself, fight back, but instead, she'd started to apologize. She was pathetic.

'Oh, let's go to sleep,' I said, turning away from her.

Soon Beverly began to breathe deeply and evenly. Every now and then, she coughed or muttered something, and sometimes, I could just make out the twitching of her limbs through the darkness. I wished I could sleep too, but my mattress sagged in the middle and I couldn't get comfortable. I wished I'd thought to bring a torch. The lamp was over Beverly's bed, and there wasn't one on my side. In such unfamiliar surroundings, I felt a bit spooked. I told myself that I was being silly; I'd slept in so many different places on tour with Mum. Why should one more new one bother me so much? I decided it had more to do with Beverly than anything else, although it was probably being confined in such a small room too.

If only Beverly had been the kind of cousin you'd be proud to have instead of a social embarrassment. As a small child, I had invented a large family for myself. I'd called them the Gordons and they'd been complete; a mother, a father, two brothers and a sister. The sister had been two years older than me but had been endlessly kind and patient. She'd protected me from every evil and had always been there to help me through new schools or tough homework. She'd looked great too, with a lovely figure and perfect clothes. I'd called her Griselda because, at five years old, I'd thought Griselda was the nicest name in the world.

Now I wished that my younger self had had a bit more taste, but having known my pretend sister Griselda for six long years, it seemed a bit late to start renaming her. Every night, before I went to sleep, I still thought of Griselda and her brothers, Gerry and Gilbert. The letter G had figured a lot because it was my own initial. There had even been a dog called Gaynor. And two sensible grandparents who'd taken me on imaginary outings to shows and circuses at Christmas and Easter. I'd rehearsed the G family sagas over and over in my head. If only Beverly and Patience could have borne some resemblance to the Gs. If only they hadn't been so peculiar.

Suddenly, just as I had feared, Beverly gave out this horrible grunting sound and then she started to snore. I hastily pictured the Gs. It was a glorious summer's day and we were all picnicking by a river. The parents watched as Griselda swam gracefully and Gilbert and Gerry threw a ball to one another. I was just dipping my toes in the water and enjoying the coolness as it washed over my feet. But every now and then, Beverly's snores intruded and the picture in my mind went blank, like a television that had been unplugged.

After fifteen minutes or so, I decided that I couldn't stand it any longer and I reached out and dug Beverly in the side with my forefinger. Beverly grunted again and turned over. The snoring ceased. The Gs began to swim again in all their glory. I climbed the highest rock and stood poised. Then I dived into the pool of bright blue water, and it was the most glorious, graceful dive ever in the history of the universe. But as I surfaced I became aware that the Gs had disappeared, and in their place was Patience, bobbing about like an overstuffed porpoise. And shivering on the edge, looking drenched and utterly miserable, stood Beverly. Then once again, the picture went blank.

Patience was singing as she stood on the doorstep the following evening. She didn't have to ring the bell; Beverly and Mikey rushed out to greet her.

'How was the conference?' asked Bev.

'Funny thing you know, speech-making,' said Patience. 'You always think you can't do it and when you get there, everything goes fine.'

'All *right*,' said Mikey.

'I'll just go up and see your mum and then Grace and I will be getting off home. It's later than I thought it would be.'

I sat on the faded sofa waiting for Patience to finish talking to Bev's mum. It was as if she was delaying on purpose. All I wanted to do was to get away from Beverly, but everything kept conspiring to keep us together for the longest possible time. I looked across the room where Beverly was sitting on a stool mending a hole in a pair of socks. She was using thin cotton thread and she was knotting it. 'That's useless,' I muttered. 'You'll get blisters.'

'You do it then,' said Beverly.

At last Gran came downstairs again. 'I think your mum's much better,' she said. Beverly beamed at her. 'I knew she was,' she boomed. I understood now why Auntie Donna was ill; it was the terrible level of noise she had to endure.

'Can we go now?' I asked. Mikey glared at me and I felt angry with myself. I kept forgetting he was there. He tended to sit quietly, just letting things happen and then all of a sudden, he'd say something that made you realize he'd been watching all the time. I had let a lot of things slip that weekend and Mikey had clocked them all. I had the most miserable feeling that he really didn't like me much.

'Say goodbye to your cousins then, and thank them for having you,' said Patience, as if I was six. I mumbled something that could have passed for thanks. It was at times like this that it was hardest to remember that Gran was Diana, the adolescent's friend.

But as we walked home, it became clear that Patience had decided to forgive me for bad-mouthing her the other day. As a sign of this, she sang as we went along the High Street. Instead of minding, and wondering if anyone could hear, I made myself remember that Patience only sang when she was happy and was with people she liked. The song-less days, when we had fallen out, had been far worse; sad and full of nothing.

Back in my own room, I was glad of my own space.

Patience said she'd start the evening meal. 'We could play some computer games later,' she added, looking at me hopefully. 'I could teach you. It's more fun with two.'

'I know how,' I lied. 'I just don't want to.'

Patience's face took on a look of abject unhappiness.

'OK, OK,' I conceded. I was remembering how empty life had been when Patience hadn't sung.

Twelve

I was awoken by the sounds of Patience singing loudly in the kitchen. It made a change for her to be up before I was and I couldn't decide whether to be pleased that we wouldn't have the usual fight for the bathroom or cross with her for disturbing my sleep. Then I remembered that I had to be at school half an hour earlier than usual because our class was going on an outing. Patience was making an effort to get me organized. Even though I didn't need anyone to sort me out, I was touched that she'd remembered and that she cared enough to make sure I got there on time. I scrambled out of bed much faster than I normally did, looking forward to the day ahead. It wasn't that I knew much about paintings or even that I liked looking at them, but a day without lessons couldn't be bad, especially when the visit would wipe out a double dose of maths.

When I got downstairs, I found that Patience had laid the breakfast table just the way I liked it. Everything was neatly ordered, and we were using proper china plates and mugs – nothing with frogs on, just the plain, grown-up stuff. I ate my toast and listened to her going on excitedly about a TV programme she'd watched the night before when I'd gone to bed. I thought it was tactless of her to be so happy about something I'd been forced to miss because of her rules about bed time. The good feelings I'd had towards her took a little dive.

She seemed to notice that I wasn't that impressed by the topic of conversation because she changed the subject. 'What will you be looking at today then, darling?' she asked.

'I'm not sure. Old paintings mostly, the stuff they did hundreds of years ago.'

Patience frowned. 'A film would be more fun,' she said. 'Or a museum where you can do things, where you don't have to just stand around, like the Science Museum.'

'There's a cartoon,' I said. 'It's by someone called Leonardo.'

'That'll be Leonardo da Vinci,' Gran answered. 'He was an inventor as well as a painter.' She seemed to know a lot for someone who thought museums and galleries were boring.

'It should be interesting,' I said. I often found myself taking the opposite view to Patience, not because I really believed it but because I felt I had to. She had such strong ideas about everything that sometimes I felt that if I didn't assert myself I'd be completely smothered by her. And also, someone had to be grown up. It seemed to me then that if we both acted like kids, there'd be nothing left but chaos.

Yet that morning, I had to admit, Patience had

behaved in a pretty grown-up way. She'd got up early in order to make me sandwiches, which she'd put in a proper sandwich box. And she'd added fresh fruit and a muesli bar, 'Because I know you worry about nutrition,' she said.

I didn't tell her that muesli bars weren't very good for you on account of all the sugar they put into them. I just said it was all absolutely excellent.

Marley came sneaking up to me and nudged my leg with the side of his face. It really irritated me when he did that, and I almost pushed him away, but then I remembered that Patience had got up early for me and had made breakfast and sorted out a packed lunch, and it seemed only fair that I should make an effort too, so I let him continue to rub. He purred very loudly and Patience and I both started laughing because he sounded exactly like an electric buzz-saw.

Patience said she'd let me walk to school alone that morning and I flashed her a grateful look. As she waved goodbye from the gate, I thought how different she was from Mum. My mother would never have made up lunch for me, she would have ordered sandwiches from some expensive caterer. There would have been anchovies, probably, and olives and I absolutely hate them. Mum had done things in a grand way, but she'd never had time to ask what I'd actually wanted.

The coach was waiting outside the school gates. Mrs Power was ushering everyone on with a lot of fuss and bother. Merle and Carol were already seated at the back, so I automatically paired off with Jess. Mrs Power decided to argue about the fact that Jess was wearing the wrong colour socks, and by the time she'd finished, two other people had nicked the seats that Merle and Carol had been trying to save for us. We were stuck near the front instead. I was disappointed, but Mrs Power was right behind, so there was nothing we could do. Carol kept digging one of the usurpers with her elbow, which made me smile. I thought it served her right.

It wasn't a very long journey, but the traffic into central London was bad, so it took twice the time it needed to. Jess told me lots of interesting things about Carol and Merle to stop us getting bored.

'Once,' she said, 'Merle locked Attila in a cupboard, the one near the art room. He nearly suffocated; there wasn't much air in there. He never found out who'd done it.'

'That must have taken guts,' I said.

'No, she's sad, really. She once told a teacher that it was me who'd taken all this stuff from the domestic science room, and I hadn't done anything, she was just saving her own skin. Gutless, that's all. Gutless. You're not gutless though, are you?'

I shook my head, though I wasn't absolutely sure. I looked across at Beverly. She was sitting next to Mrs Power – no one else would have her. She seemed to be enjoying herself. She was talking and laughing in that hideous honking way of hers. 'I'll tell you who is gutless,' I said. 'Beverly Boot Lick. Just listen to her!'

But Jess carried on as if I hadn't spoken. 'Carol isn't as brave as she makes out, I can tell you that much,' she said. 'I do half the stuff everyone thinks she does, but she takes all the credit. It was me who fought those Year Nine boys when they tried to take our money off us, not her, she just stood there, but she said it was all down to her. And I'll tell you another thing . . .'

Jess told me a good many other things, until I wasn't sure what or who to believe. It was an uncomfortable feeling, but I didn't let on. Jess was too interesting a storyteller. And I needed to know what was what. When you're new, you have a lot of catching up to do, I was all too aware of that.

The coach dropped us all off outside the gallery and then departed. I stood beside Jess, rubbing my leg. I was getting cramp from all the sitting I'd been doing. Now that we were there, I had a horrible feeling this outing was going to be just like lessons, and the feeling deepened as we were welcomed by our guide and given worksheets. Carol immediately made hers into a paper dart and got frowned at by all the grown-ups in sight. She assumed her most virtuous expression but nobody was fooled. 'Carol Wilson and Merle Gray, come and stand beside me now,' Mrs Power ordered. Carol faked deafness but for once Mrs Power wasn't deceived, and they were forced to trail along beside her and Beverly while Jess and I played Spot the Bare Lady to pass the time.

The best thing about the gallery was that there

were lots of opportunities for this. Most of the pictures had people without any clothes on, but it was called Art, so it wasn't seen as rude. Me and Jess were a bit childish that afternoon, although we didn't see ourselves as childish at the time. We thought we were being grown up and sophisticated and it was a great feeling. I wound up laughing so much that I had to sit down in one of their big squishy seats, the kind that makes you sound as if you've got a bad case of wind as you land. This, of course, made us laugh even more, and in the end, we got a big telling off from Mrs Power too, even worse than the one Merle and Carol had got. Beverly the Good just stood there looking smug. I really hated her then. When no one could see, I gave her a good sharp pinch just to teach her a lesson. She squealed and everybody turned to look. She didn't know who'd done it, though the grin across my face nearly gave me away.

I quite liked some of the colours of the paintings, but I wasn't really in the mood for art. It was a warm day and I wanted to be outside. Trafalgar Square was just a few yards away and it would have been more fun to have seen the fountains or perhaps to have fed the pigeons. Mum would have been disappointed in me. She would have said it was time I started to act my age. She expected me to like what she called Culture, though she included African stuff in this, not just all the things that come from England. Patience wouldn't have approved of the bare lady game, but otherwise, she would have been proud of me, I think. She wanted me to act my age too, but with her, it was wanting me to behave younger, not older. Patience would have liked the way I was being more like a child.

Sometimes, it seemed quite confusing, having a mother who wanted me to behave one way and a gran who wanted me to do the opposite. In my worst nightmares, I imagined living with both of them at the same time, forever pulled in opposite directions, never knowing who to please.

We ate lunch in Trafalgar Square though and it was fun, chucking bits of bread around for the pigeons to eat. One sat right on my hand and pecked at the last piece of sandwich I was holding. I was nervous that it would bite or something, so I shook it away, but Carol let one sit on her head without even blinking.

We did see the Leonardo Cartoon, but it wasn't anything like I'd imagined. It wasn't animated at all, it was just a line drawing. That's what cartoon meant in the old days. I was pretty disappointed. But then the guide took us into this big room where there were easels and things and we were allowed to copy from some posters and also to make up our own drawings using coloured pastels. I'd never liked drawing much until then, but she made it really lively and I started doing things I'd never been able to draw before. I glanced across at Jess, Carol and Merle. They were still messing about, so their paper was just a blank space, but mine was full of life and colour. I began to think about the pictures I'd seen in a different way. It was both harder and easier to draw than I'd imagined and I really started to enjoy myself. I told Jess that she should try it, but she just laughed at me. I think she thought I was showing off.

The tutor came round to see what we'd done and she said 'good' twice about mine. Beverly got told good too, but only the once. She hadn't done any rubbing out at all, her drawing looked neat and ordered, though it wasn't as good as mine. I sat back, feeling pleased. I asked if we could keep our pictures and the tutor said yes. I rolled up mine carefully and made sure it didn't get squashed as we got on the coach. I was going to show it to Patience. She'd be impressed. She seemed to enjoy looking at the things I did, and she never got bored; she never said she was too busy or too tired the way my mum always had.

There was music coming through the speakers on the journey back so nobody talked much. It had been a very full day. Carol started singing and a few other people joined in, but I was content to doze.

Jess poked me in the ribs. 'Show us your picture again.'

'Why?' I said. She'd seen it twice already.

'I just want a look.'

Her interest made me suspicious. 'No,' I said.

'Oh, go on,' she insisted.

'No,' I repeated, too drowsy to care what she thought of me. Jess suddenly lunged and snatched the rolled up picture from my side. I grabbed hold of it and the corner tore off in her hand. 'Look what you've done!' I shouted at her.

'Keep calm, it was only an accident,' she said.

I thought over what had happened, trying to decide if she'd meant to upset me or not. I couldn't figure it out, so I gave her the benefit of the doubt, but inside, I continued to wonder. I wasn't really sure of Jess; or Carol or Merle, come to that. It was a worrying feeling. I spent the rest of the coach journey in silence.

Thirteen

Mum phoned on the Monday of the following week. 'It was great to get your letter. How's school? Are you still enjoying it?' she asked.

'It's OK,' I said.

'And you're settling down all right?'

I hesitated. It wasn't exactly a private conversation – Patience was sitting close by, reading one of the books that she'd persuaded me to lend her. 'It's great, I can't wait to find out how the family survives,' she kept saying, even though the story had been written for twelve-year-olds.

'Grace?' said Mum.

'It's all OK,' I said. I wished I could tell her that I hated it, because then she might come and get me, but the truth was, I didn't mind it all that much. My days were nice and predictable on the whole, apart from Patience's eccentricities, and I was finding that there was something very comforting about having a regular existence and spending most of your time in just one place. Jess and Merle were my friends, and Carol was quite nice to me most of the time. Since she was hardly ever polite to anyone, I took this as a positive sign. And even Patience was bearable now that I was starting to get used to her. If only Mum could be there too, I believed I might really start to be happy. 'I wish you weren't so far away,' I said.

'Me too, darling, me too,' she answered. 'Grace, have you remembered it's your gran's birthday soon?'

'Yes,' I replied softly. How could I forget? Patience had been dropping some very unsubtle hints for days and she'd even decided to have a party. Apart from the fact that it would mean spending more time with Beverly, it was worrying to think how embarrassing this might be. 'I want lots of balloons in the brightest colours,' Patience kept saying. 'And a big chocolate cake in the shape of a frog. I've ordered one specially from the bakers in the High Street. Huge it is, so everyone will get a big piece.' I could hear her voice in my head even as I was talking to Mum. 'She's got a frog cake,' I said.

Mum tutted but all she said was, 'And you'll be sure to get her something nice?'

'Yes,' I answered.

'I'm sending her a woollen shawl. It's made of mohair and it'll keep her warm.'

I thought how much Patience would hate a woollen shawl. Didn't Mum know her at all? 'I don't think she'd like that, Mum,' I said.

'Why on earth not?'

'She isn't that old,' I whispered, hoping Patience wouldn't realize we were still talking about her.

'I know she isn't, I just thought it would be cosy for her. Anyway, it's too late, I put it in the post this morning.'

'*Mum!*'

'She'll love it, really she will. It's orange, with fuchsia pink sparkly bits.'

I decided that if it was in Gran's favourite colours, it might not be such a disaster. As I hung up the phone, I wondered what I could buy for Patience. The obvious present was some sort of frog, but all frogs looked the same to me, I didn't think I'd manage to find one that Patience didn't have already. What would Beverly be giving her? She was sure to find something that Patience really wanted. She was bound to emerge as the favourite grandchild.

Patience's birthday fell on a Saturday, which was very convenient for parties, she said. I was up early as usual that morning, and expected Gran to be late down – she generally slept till eleven or longer at weekends. But at half-past seven, she came downstairs, singing at full volume and with a beaming smile. 'Good morning, good morning, good morning,' she said.

'Hi,' I said. Patience looked at me expectantly, but I pretended not to notice.

'Any post?'

'Hasn't come yet.'

'You sure?'

'Sure and certain.'

Patience looked disappointed. 'Well, I'd better get myself a special breakfast, seeing how this is a special day.'

I assumed a puzzled look and went on sipping my orange juice.

'I needed a good, early start. I have to get ready for the party this afternoon.'

I clapped my hand to my mouth and uttered a cry. 'Oh, Gran! I forgot all about it!'

Patience looked sad for a moment, but then she said, 'Oh well, never mind, it doesn't really matter. I mean, I know you were busy this week with homework and all.' Her voice was tight and the words forced. She tried to smile, but I could see it was an effort.

I gave in then. 'Fooled you!' I said, and I ran to the drawer. I pulled out the present I'd just hidden there. 'Happy birthday,' I said.

Patience gave one of her enormous, never-ending laughs. 'Oh, Grace,' she sighed as the tears of merriment ran down her face, 'you really got me going that time.'

'Open it, go on,' I said.

'Frog paper!'

'I knew you'd like that.'

Gran began to tear the paper off and then remembered that it might be possible to salvage the frogs, so she went at it more slowly and carefully, so as not to rip the wrapping. 'Frog place mats!' said Patience, pulling them out of the paper with a sigh of true happiness.

'You haven't got them already, have you?' I asked anxiously.

'No, I've never even seen them until now,' said Patience. 'They're so beautiful.'

I looked down at the mats I'd found quite by chance when I'd been looking for a frog plate or mug. Beautiful wasn't quite how I'd have described them. The frogs seemed more like toads; they had bulging eyes and a particularly slimy look; certainly, they were likely to put most people off their food. But at least Patience liked them, and that was the main thing.

The morning went by so quickly that I began to worry that we wouldn't be ready in time for the party. Gran went outside and tied four balloons in pink, orange, red and yellow to the gatepost. Two had Happy Birthday written on them. I cringed.

Inside, Patience hung streamers and laid out cardboard hats and some of the crackers left over from Christmas.

'Is it just children coming then?' I asked.

Patience looked surprised. 'No, it's all my friends, children and grown-ups as well.'

I fell silent. This was going to be a very strange party. I would never have had one as childish as this, and I wasn't even twelve.

'OK, time for my party frock,' said Patience. 'What will you be wearing?'

'What I'm wearing now,' I said.

Patience looked at my jeans and zipped-front

sweatshirt. 'You don't feel in the party mood?' she asked.

The honest answer was no, not in the least, but I just said, 'I bet all the other kids will dress like this. Nowadays, you just wear ordinary sorts of clothes, nothing too fancy or you just look silly.'

'Seems to me that you worry about looking silly way too much,' Patience replied as she went upstairs to change.

I waited nervously at the foot of the stairs, trying to figure out what Gran's idea of a party frock might be. As Patience descended, I knew I'd been right to be worried. She was wearing a bright red frilly number with a stiff underskirt and matching red shoes. She resembled a postbox.

'Oh, Gran!' I breathed.

Patience mistook my sigh of disbelief for a sigh of wonder. She beamed. I didn't have the heart to disillusion her.

'You sure you don't want to nice yourself up for this party?' she asked. 'I mean if everyone else is dressed up, you might look out of place.'

'It's OK, really.'

Patience sniffed as if to say that she didn't see how anyone could go to a party dressed like that.

'My sentiments exactly,' I muttered, looking again at Gran's red frock.

But as the guests began to pass excitedly through the decorated gate, I started to understand what Patience had meant. Everyone was dressed to kill. And they were all wearing the most garish colours they could lay their hands on. Even Uncle James had a purple suit, which he claimed to have borrowed from Mikey. And as for Beverly, she was dressed in the most putrid shade of lilac. But the biggest shock of all was to see Mrs Harcourt coming through the door in a salmon-pink taffeta piece with pale yellow spots. I blinked, blinked again and stepped aside to let her pass, rendered speechless by the sheer glow of it.

Patience had invited a wide range of people to the party; she seemed to have friends from every part of the world. I was afraid that some of the white people there would look down on her and think she was stupid for having this kind of party, but no one seemed to think it was odd at all, they all seemed to be out to enjoy themselves. Everyone had brought a present. They'd gone to a lot of trouble; each was packaged in brightly printed paper, and some were tied with bows. Patience exclaimed over each one, and every time she unwrapped another frog or a book about frogs or a frog-shaped cushion, she claimed it was the very thing she'd dreamed of having. Beverly handed over her present with a pleased expression, as if she knew she'd hit on the best possible gift. Patience unwrapped it quickly. I couldn't believe it. She'd got a set of frog place mats, identical to the ones I'd given her that very morning!

Patience looked miserable too for the briefest moment, as if she knew how disappointed each of us would be. Then she beamed again and said, 'I'm having a dozen people round to dinner the week after next, and I so wanted to set the table with my frog place mats. Now, thanks to both of you, I'll be able to.'

Beverly looked confused, so Patience explained about my present, insisting all the while that it didn't matter in the least, it was actually the best possible turn events could have taken.

I was furious. How dare Beverly undo all the effort I'd made by getting Patience the exact same present! It was as if she'd done it on purpose. 'You should take it back to the shop, get Gran something else instead,' I told Beverly.

'No, I'm very happy with both, I really am,' said Patience.

'Why should I take mine back? You take yours back,' replied Beverly.

'Mine were the first ones. That's why mine should stay.'

'Girls, please,' said Mrs Harcourt. 'This is meant to be a party, not a battle ground.'

We both subsided, feeling conspicuous and disappointed. I think we'd each wanted to give Gran a special present and each of us felt let down by the way it had turned out.

'You know, you two really should try to make friends,' said Patience. 'You even have the same taste.'

I wasn't sure which was more insulting, the idea that I actually liked frogs or the idea that me and Beverly were in any sense the same.

Patience put an arm round each of us. 'Come on

folks, let's party!' she said, and then she pulled the cling film off the food like a magician revealing the rabbit in the hat.

I was bored within minutes. Everyone was either too young or too old. Patience put on her favourite music and, as we ate and drank, everybody danced. I watched Mrs Harcourt put on a cone-shaped hat with elastic underneath her chin and realized there was no end to the foolishness grown-ups were prepared to indulge in. I thought back to the times I'd wanted to be grown up and immediately took it all back. Adults were cringe-making, it was better to be a kid by miles. They never seemed to realize how pathetic they looked, especially when they danced with a slice of frog cake in one hand and a cup of Diet Coke in the other.

I decided that I wanted to go home, and then I remembered I was home already. I knew I'd have to stay and watch people making bigger and bigger idiots of themselves.

Beverly was teaching a man who looked at least eighty-five how to play Rampage. He seemed to be having the time of his life. Uncle James was eating the largest pile of orange jelly ever to have hit a plate. And Mikey was setting up a video of *Tom and Jerry* for all those who were interested. I was shocked when half the people in the room decided to watch.

In the end, I went upstairs for some peace and quiet, but my bed was covered with a giant Snakes and Ladders board, and five people over fifty were shouting that they'd better not land on that big fat snake. I opened the door to the bathroom and found that two grown-ups and a kid had filled the bath and were floating some of Gran's prize frogs. I ran downstairs to give her the news.

'They've got your frogs, they're making them float in water.'

Patience just smiled. 'That's what frogs do.'

'But they're getting wet.'

'Chill, Grace, it's cool,' said Gran.

I ground my teeth. I hated it when Patience tried to speak like a young person.

I let myself out into the small backyard. There was no grass in it but Gran had planted some flowers in pots and they were coming into bloom. It was a cold day, so I knew I was likely to have the space to myself. I sat on the crazy paving. It almost froze my butt off, but it was better than being indoors.

Then suddenly the back door opened. Someone was coming out to join me. It was Beverly. Was there no escape? I turned my head away and tried to look as unwelcoming as possible, but she didn't take the hint. She sat down beside me.

'It's cold,' she said.

'Better go indoors then.'

'What are you doing?'

'Just sitting here. By myself.'

'It's a nice little garden, isn't it?' She'd brought a plate of crisps and cakes out with her. She offered some to me, but I didn't want anything she'd mauled first. I didn't look at her. I knew she was probably chewing with her mouth open. 'It's OK that we bought the same thing for Gran,' she said. 'She's pleased, she's glad she's got two sets. Then when one wears out, she'll have the other one.'

'Place mats don't wear out.'

'They do,' boomed Beverly. 'Mum had some once, and the pictures got all scratched and chipped.'

'Not for years.' Then I realized I was sounding as if I minded that we'd got the same, so I added, 'Anyway, I don't care. It isn't important.' Of course, the last thing you should do when you mind something is tell people you don't care. They always see through it, and then they feel sorry for you.

Beverly said, 'I suppose I could take mine back.'

'No! If she wants them both, let her have them both. I told you, I don't care!'

I ran back inside the house. Everyone was still jigging about to the music. Mrs Harcourt was doing something that looked like the twist. I'd seen it in a film once. It was a dance they'd had in the old days and it made you look a complete moron, especially if the upper part of your body stayed still the way Mrs Harcourt's did.

I went to see what food was left, but it was mostly crumbs. I didn't care though. I wasn't very hungry anyway. In the end, the only place I could find that was safe from all the gruesomeness of grown-ups acting like children was the cupboard under the stairs. I made myself some coffee and took it in there with a set of magazines. I didn't come out again until after they'd played Musical Bumps and Pass the Parcel.

Fourteen

Patience and I were washing up after the party. 'Why don't you get a dishwasher?' I said to her.

'For one person?'

'There's me as well, or at least at the moment, there is.'

Patience put down the tea towel and said, 'You know, when Odette first said to me that she'd like you to come and live here, I didn't think it was a good idea. I didn't think it would work out.'

This surprised me. I'd imagined that Patience had jumped at the chance of having her favourite grandchild for a long visit. 'Why not?' I asked.

'Well, I'm a bit set in my ways you know. And I'm used to having a lot of space.'

'And you don't like me being in the bathroom when you need to go in there.'

Patience grinned. 'It isn't always easy, sharing things.'

'But you used to share with Grandad.'

'Yes, but once he died, I got used to being on my own.'

'How do you feel about it now?' I asked.

In answer, Patience put her arms around me and gave me a hug.

I think those first weeks had been difficult for both of us. Mum was so different from Gran; Mum was quieter and not so obvious about everything. I liked people who moved softly and I preferred it when people talked and laughed quietly. My favourite colours were black and brown and dark red. I didn't like brightness: if I'd chosen the decor in Gran's house, I'd have had it subtle and sophisticated. I liked gentle music: classical, mainly, and I liked quite sensible television programmes. Gran and I were opposites in most respects and it seemed to me that opposites didn't always attract.

Patience began to put the cups and plates away in the cupboard. It made a change to have the kitchen looking tidy. Normally, although it was always clean, it was chaotic like most of her surroundings. It was difficult to fit all the crockery in, because Gran had been given a number of froggy items for her birthday. There were two more mugs, two cereal bowls, and even little frog-shaped salt and pepper pots. I thought again about the disastrous place mats. I was still fuming. Trust Beverly to mess up something else for me. I really was sick and tired of her.

'You know, it was a very nice birthday,' said Patience.

I nodded, though it hadn't seemed that nice to me.

'You didn't play Pass the Parcel, and I'd done it up so tight with so many layers, it broke Mary's fingernails.'

'Mrs Harcourt played Pass the Parcel?'

'Everyone played except you,' said Gran, with a note of reproach in her voice.

'I thought it was silly,' I said. Then, out of curiosity, I asked who won. It was bound to have been Beverly. Gran would probably have stopped the music on purpose when the parcel reached her so that she would get it.

'Fred Morton won. A lovely pen, it was.'

He was the man Beverly had taught to play Rampage. At least Gran hadn't fixed the game, that was something. But as soon as I thought it, she said, 'I knew he needed a pen. You can't get much on a pension, it all goes on food.'

'You let him win?' I said in disbelief.

'I didn't see the harm,' said Gran.

Marley came through the cat flap then and jumped on to the kitchen table. 'Off there,' said Patience, but it was totally without conviction, so Marley continued to stay where he was. I hate it when animals get on the furniture, so I shouted at him, 'Get down, Marley!' and he jumped off straight away. I was pleased with myself. Grace Oswald, obedience trainer *extraordinaire*.

'It's funny, he always does what you say,' said Patience.

'Not always,' I admitted. I still hadn't managed to stop him sleeping in my bed whenever the bedroom door was open, and I *really* shouted at him then.

Marley didn't seem to take offence though. In fact, he seemed to like me. He began to rub his side against my leg and started purring. Against my better judgement, I stroked him gently from his back to his tail. He purred even louder then.

Patience looked delighted, as if something really special had happened. OK, so I wasn't threatening to kill the cat, but it was no big deal.

I offered to make us some hot chocolate. Since the weekend with Beverly, I'd started training myself to help a bit around the house. My pride wouldn't let me stay useless – it was too embarrassing.

We took our drinks into the living room and sat in front of the gas fire, which sent out a warm red glow. Marley insisted on sitting on my lap, and just for once, I didn't push him off. A few fleas probably wouldn't kill me.

It was kind of cosy, sitting there with Gran. 'I had such a nice day,' she said again, and although it irritated me to have her repeat everything all the time, I did quite like her enthusiasm. She never behaved as if she was bored or fed up, she always enjoyed things, even silly things (especially silly things, come to think of it) and her happiness was often catching.

'Why don't we do something nice tomorrow?' she said.

'Such as what?'

'Go see a film, maybe.'

I remembered that Patience had taken Beverly to

a multiplex. I didn't want to be outdone, so I said, 'OK, but to a really big cinema, yeah?'

'Yeah,' agreed Patience happily.

Another good thing about Patience was that she always did things in style. She wasn't extravagant; we didn't take taxis anywhere when a bus would do, but she certainly wasn't mean. When you went out with her, she did everything to make it a really good day.

We took the bus to the West End, and went to a cinema in Leicester Square. Patience tried to let me choose the film but it didn't quite work out that way. There were three films that were suitable for my age group, she said; one was called *Space Station*, the second was a Cops and Robbers thing, and the third was about a girl musician, a child genius, who struggles to cope with her gift. I wanted to see the one about music. I'd often wished that I'd been really musical because then I could have followed in Mum's footsteps. Whenever she'd taken me to a concert or a rehearsal or to meet friends of hers, they'd always assumed that I had at least some of her talent. Only I didn't, to be honest. I could sing in key, but my voice was nothing special, just average. I couldn't imagine myself ever performing on stage, either. I tend to get self-conscious, a bit like Beverly when she's reading. So opera certainly wasn't for me, but I didn't know what was. Sometimes I had this awful suspicion that I might be totally useless, worse than Beverly even, and it was a fear that kept me awake at night. So, having pictured myself in my most secret fantasies as a virtuoso singer or violinist or conductor, I wanted to see a film about just such a child prodigy.

'Oh,' said Patience, when I named my choice, and her face fell.

'Isn't that the one you wanted to see then?' I asked.

'I don't mind,' said Gran, in just the sort of tone that suggested that she did mind very much.

'Which would you have gone for then?'

'It isn't my choice,' she replied, obviously struggling with herself.

'But if it was your choice,' I persisted.

'Well . . . if it was my choice, I'd want to see something exciting, with some special effects.'

'Like *Space Station*?'

'A bit like that, yes,' said Patience.

'OK, we'll see that one then,' I said.

'But you wanted to see the other one.'

'It doesn't matter, really.'

'I said you could choose though,' Patience replied.

'Well, I am choosing. I choose *Space Station*,' I answered.

Once in the foyer, we got everything: popcorn, drinks, a box of chocolates, and the promise of an ice cream later. In the past, when I'd been taken to a film, by Mum or one of her friends, it had always been either/or; you can have either popcorn *or* a drink *or* ice cream. There was too much of everything with Patience, though of course, I hardly had any; Patience munched her way through most of it. But my appetite was small by comparison, so I didn't mind that much.

The film wasn't a bad choice, as it turned out, although the one about music would have interested me more. This was an all-action shoot-the-alien sort of drama, full of flashing lights and heroes.

Patience got so excited in the tense bits that she let out little squeals every now and then. I did try to pretend I wasn't with her, but I didn't feel quite as mortified as usual. For one thing, it was dark, so no one could really tell who I was with. And for another, I was getting used to her, and I didn't mind what she did quite so much any more.

When the film finished, and the lights went up, Patience let out a happy sigh. '*Marvellous*,' she said.

She tucked her arm into mine and we walked out of the cinema feeling contented.

Outside, there was someone selling string puppets. He got them to jump about and bend down and it was quite entertaining. Gran insisted on getting me one. I didn't really feel like having it; they were meant for someone younger than almost twelve, I think, but it was nice, getting a souvenir of the day and kind of Gran to buy it for me. Besides, it was hard to argue with her. She always assumed that when you said no to something it was because you were worried about the expense. It never seemed to occur to her that maybe you just didn't want it.

I was sleepy on the way home, so I dozed while we were on the bus, leaning against Gran. She felt comfy and safe; a bit like the teddy I'd had as a child.

Fifteen

I was bouncing a ball against the wall and then trying to shoot it into the basketball net. So far, I'd managed two baskets out of three, so I was feeling quite pleased with myself. I wished Carol would hurry up and join me though. She'd been put in detention for talking in class throughout the previous day. I don't know why I'd been left out of it. I'd been talking too, but somehow I was less noticeable than she was.

Suddenly she came running out. She had large hands and feet, but she always moved gracefully. I just stood and watched as she came towards me. She seemed excited about something. She skidded to a halt beside me, dropped her bag and intercepted the ball I was bouncing. Then she galloped along the concrete and zinged it effortlessly into the net. She turned to me with a pleased expression on her face and gave a little bow.

'Not bad,' I said. Carol was conceited enough as it was.

She raised an eyebrow. 'I'd have said brilliant, myself.'

'Your trumpeter dead then?' I asked her. It was

a phrase my mum always used when she thought I was getting above myself.

Carol ignored this and said, 'I know something you don't know.'

It was a sad fact that Carol knew an awful lot that I didn't know. In those past few weeks I'd been discovering that she was very clever indeed, though she tried not to show it. I just sighed and looked at her. I'd already learned that it was fatal to show an interest in any secret Carol had. If she thought you really wanted to be told something, she'd tantalize you with it for days. On the other hand, if you played it cool, she'd get bored and tell you with the minimal amount of teasing.

'I bet you really want to know what it is.'

I just shrugged my indifference.

'It's about you.'

'About me?' I asked, forgetting not to care. 'Honest?'

Carol gave me such a satisfied look that I felt like pounding her. Instead, I went back to indifference as fast as I could.

'Your gran's called Patience, isn't she?'

'She might be,' I said.

'You won't believe what she's done. It's in this paper.' Carol pulled out a copy of a newspaper. 'Your gran's written something.'

'What are you talking about?' I was cross with Carol now. I didn't want to have to play silly games to find out about something my own gran had done. 'Just tell me,' I said. Then I felt a bit scared, because

Carol wasn't the sort of person it was wise to be angry with. She could be pretty mean when she wanted to be.

But suddenly she gave in, and handed me the newspaper. 'Page eight in the leisure section,' she said.

I flicked rapidly through the pages. I scanned page eight, but I couldn't see anything of interest.

'The first column,' said Carol. 'Look who it's by.'

I looked properly then, and saw that Patience Oswald had written the article.

'Incredible, isn't it?' said Carol.

I felt full of warmth towards my friend. She seemed so excited by the fact that Gran was a published writer. 'Patience does loads of that sort of stuff,' I explained to her. 'Don't tell anyone, but she does a page in *Maribeth*, the problem page. She's Dear Diana.'

Carol scarcely seemed to hear. 'Yes, but look what it says in the article. You have to read it. It's about you.'

My fingers suddenly started to shake. I began to read silently. Patience Oswald was writing about someone she called Angel. She was meant to be the granddaughter of a friend, but you didn't need to be a genius to know that it was me she was talking about. This grandchild had suddenly appeared from nowhere and was staying with her gran. She disapproved of everything. She wanted to take taxis everywhere and she thought that everybody in the world should have a dishwasher. She looked down her nose at grown-ups who had parties. She hated computer games, she thought they were boring. And she said her gran was fat and old and stupid. It was meant to be funny; Angel was someone to laugh at and to despise. Altogether, she was a complete pain in the butt.

I sat on the ground, trying to take in what I was reading. How could Gran do this to me? How could she put me in a story and make me so horrible? And if Carol knew Angel was me, even though the name was different, everybody else would know too. It was the most embarrassing moment of my life.

Carol began to laugh. 'You should see your face,' she said.

I turned away from her. 'This isn't me,' I told her. 'It isn't anything like me. Anyway, it says she's the granddaughter of a friend. It isn't me, I tell you.'

'But you said your gran had a party and that it was awful. And you told me you had to wash up all the time and that you should get a dishwasher like Merle's got.'

I wished I'd never told Carol anything about my life. 'But Angel isn't me,' I repeated. 'It's poetic licence, you know, we got told about it in English. You don't tell things like they are when you're writing something, you embellish them, to make a more interesting poem or a story.'

'If you ask me, she hasn't had to do much embellishing. It's *you*, I tell you. Of course it is, it stands out a mile.'

I picked up the ball and began to run with it.

Carol didn't realize that I was trying to escape, she thought I wanted to play. She began to chase me. I kept on running though, right through the school gate. When I glanced back, I saw Carol standing still and staring after me as if she didn't understand what was going on. Once I'd reached the point where there was no possibility that she would catch up with me, I sat on the bench near the bus shelter and looked at the article again. I was hoping that maybe I'd got it wrong and that I was just imagining the similarity between Angel and me, but as I went through it I saw that if anything, it was worse than I'd first supposed. Angel even looked like me. We had the same taste in clothes too; she liked dark, muted colours and she despised brightness.

It hurt to think that Gran could make fun of me in public. Up until then, I'd been stupid enough to get it into my head that she cared about me – loved me even – yet here she was, encouraging other people to see me as stupid. I'd been quite proud of the way she'd answered the letters on the Dear Diana page. She'd been kind and understanding in her writing then. But her newspaper articles were different. They weren't understanding in the least. They showed that Patience had no idea what it was really like to be almost twelve, even though she acted so young all the time.

I think that what I felt most was a terrible sense of being let down. I'd relied on my gran, in a way, although I'd been careful not to let it show. I'd felt safe and secure with her, even more, sometimes, than I had with Mum, because my gran was always around and not in rehearsals or at grown-ups' parties. But now it was clear that Patience wasn't to be trusted at all. She was just like all the other grown-ups, she pretended to care and *said* that she cared, but it was only words.

I started to cry, I couldn't help myself. I felt so humiliated. And on top of that, I'd have to go home and face her, knowing that although she was always saying how great I was, she really thought I was a snotty little cow. I didn't want to go back, not ever, but it was cold out and I was hungry too. I searched my pockets and managed to find a pound. There was a fish and chip shop on the corner so I went inside, but as soon as I reached the counter, I was hit by the smell of pies and fish and I realized I wasn't hungry at all. In fact, I felt as if I'd never be hungry again.

'What can I get you, love?' asked the woman who was serving.

'It's all right, I've changed my mind,' I said.

'Maybe you should eat something, you look a bit peaky,' she replied, but I didn't answer, I just turned round and went back outside.

I walked home very slowly, taking care to prolong every second. It must have taken me at least half an hour.

'You're very late,' said Patience, as I walked through the front door. She must have been watching for me from the window, because she was standing in the hall to meet me.

I ignored her completely and ran upstairs, dropping the newspaper as I went. I didn't bother to pick it up – I never wanted to see it again. I went into my room and pushed the chest of drawers in front of the door so that if she took it into her head to follow me up, she wouldn't be able to get in. I took off my school uniform and changed into my usual, dull and boring dark red top and black jeans. Next I put on some music, increasing the volume, but then I remembered that everything I did was likely to turn up in the Little Angel column. The only way to hinder Gran was to do nothing at all. If I just sat on my bed and didn't make any noise – if I didn't even speak – there'd be nothing at all for her to write about ever again.

But of course, I soon became aware that even doing nothing was no solution, because Patience would probably write about that. In the next article, she'd be going on about Angel's withdrawal from the world, and telling everyone that it was typical behaviour for someone of her age.

I don't know how long I sat there, wondering what to do. I started crying again, but I was very quiet about it because I didn't want Patience to hear. If she did, that would probably go in the Little Angel column too, and everyone would think I was a big cry-baby.

Then Gran started knocking on the door. 'Grace, is anything wrong?' she said.

I stopped sniffing and went completely still and quiet.

'Grace, are you OK?'

'Fine,' I said.

'You don't sound it. Do tell me what's wrong. Maybe I could help. A trouble shared is a trouble halved, as they say.'

'Go away,' I said.

And then I was saved because the phone rang. I could hear Patience talking to someone. I soon worked out that it was Beverly. Gran started asking her if anything had happened to upset me at school. No, I thought, please don't bring Beverly into this, please. And then a terrible coldness hit me all over. Beverly probably knew about the Little Angel stuff. Maybe she'd even helped Gran to write it. They were always doing things together and giggling about them. Maybe Beverly was behind the whole thing . . .

I began to rock slowly to and fro on my bed. This was getting worse and worse, it had an unreal feeling about it, like when you were ill and had a temperature.

The house went quiet again. Then I heard Patience coming up the stairs. She knocked on the door once more. 'Grace, are you still in there?' she said.

I didn't reply, but instead of just forgetting about it and going to study her frog collection, Patience started to push open the door.

'What's going on?' she said. 'Are you trying to keep me out of your room?' She sounded half puzzled, half amused. Another piece of strange behaviour for her to write about, as if her own behaviour couldn't fill ten newspapers a week.

Then I think she must have seen the copy of the newspaper that I'd dropped as I'd come upstairs because she said, in a kind voice, 'Grace, let me in. I can explain about the article, it wasn't meant to upset you, you weren't meant to see it. Let me in, Grace.'

I didn't open the door. I felt too raw inside. And there wasn't any explanation that Gran could give that would make this right. She'd let me down. No, that wasn't a strong enough way of putting it. She'd betrayed me, and I wasn't going to forgive her for it, not ever.

Sixteen

It had been some days since I'd even spoken to Patience. She'd made me out to be some kind of little monster, and whenever I looked at anyone, on a train or a bus or just walking along the High Street, I wondered if they ever read the Little Angel column, and whether, by some act of telepathy, they knew that Angel was really me. It was hard to look anyone in the eye, especially now that Carol had told them at school.

But, to my surprise, I found that far from thinking how bad I was, the other kids were making me into a kind of celebrity. They actually thought I did *all* the things that Angel did, instead of just a few of them. Merle kept looking at me with admiration, and even Carol seemed impressed.

It was Wednesday afternoon, the time when my class had a basketball session. I'd picked up the basics of the game at some of the other schools I'd attended, so already I could play pretty well. I was one of the taller ones, and I never seemed to have any trouble getting the ball in the basket. Me, Carol, Jess and Merle had been put in the same team, and we were probably the best players in the lower school. Even though she was quite small, Jess could pass and get baskets as well as anyone. We were all tipped to be chosen for matches next season, when we were old enough, but this was just a practice game. The only snag was that Beverly was on our team too, though it seemed like she was playing for the opposition.

'Come on, Beverly!' we all kept shouting at her.

'Useless!' one of us would say, and then Beverly would be even more inclined to stand still, doing nothing.

Patrick Matthews, who had fair hair and buck teeth, said, 'You'd think she'd be able to do it, wouldn't you? All the other black kids can play properly. What's the matter with her?'

I couldn't decide what I thought about this. He'd said exactly what I was thinking; Beverly was letting down me, Jess, Carol and Merle by being so useless. And yet at the same time, a little voice inside me was saying, we don't have to be good at anything just because we're black, it's stupid, it shouldn't be like that.

I actually think that Beverly could have been a good player if she'd wanted to. She was quite a fast runner, even though her style was ungainly and she waddled and flapped her arms like a turkey trying to avoid the oven. She could catch well, and throw straight, and you don't really need a whole lot more to be at least OK. But Beverly just didn't try. She dreamed all the time. When she should have been concentrating on the ball, she stood staring into space. When she should have tried to shoot it into the basket, she tossed it to one of the other members of the team and it was nearly always intercepted and lost. It seemed to me that she was messing up the game on purpose and I really wanted to win. The sight of Beverly being so pathetic and lousing up the match for the rest of us made me so mad that I could hardly see straight. And of course, because we were cousins, her uselessness reflected on me. If I didn't watch out, everyone would start to think that being no good was a family trait.

Mrs Summers, the games teacher, was also losing patience with her. She kept saying, 'Run, girl, run, don't just stand there.' Then she added, 'And tie your shoelaces, Beverly. Do you want to fall flat on your face?'

Carol glared at Bev, who was still just standing there. 'She's not even trying,' she said, for everyone to hear.

'I'm the person who decides who's trying and who isn't round here,' Mrs Summers replied, and she blew on the whistle for us to continue the game.

And then suddenly, Beverly was beside me, looking feeble and as if she didn't know a ball from a blade of grass. I might have been Little Angel at that moment. Every grievance I had against Beverly rushed to the surface. She was stupid. She dressed like she lived on the streets. She didn't speak, she shouted. Her exercise books were grubby and smudged. She snored. She was seen as special by Patience. She'd bought her frog place mats. She had two parents and a brother. And worst of all, we were related.

So, as Beverly fumbled yet another shot, I glanced quickly at Mrs Summers. She was telling Louise Flaxe to stop talking to Thomas and concentrate on the game. It was the perfect opportunity. I slammed my whole body into Beverly. She toppled over and went down sharply on her knees. As she tried to stand, I saw that her legs were all scraped and bloody. There was a brief moment of satisfaction as I saw the cousin from hell get what she deserved. And then, briefer still, there was a moment of regret as I saw the hurt look on Beverly's face.

Mrs Summers assumed it was an accident. 'I told you to do up your trainers, Beverly,' she said, and then she proceeded to tear her off a strip for being so careless. I could tell from their expressions that Carol, Jess, and Merle knew what I'd done, but the funny part was, nobody else saw, or at least, no one admitted to seeing a thing. The other team just looked at Beverly and listened to the telling off she got, excited at having a ringside seat at a so-called accident.

More than anything, I felt pleased with myself. If Beverly even tried to tell Mrs Summers that I'd pushed her, it would seem as if she was trying to put the blame on someone else for her own carelessness. She just couldn't win. Carol said, '*Gotcha!*' under her breath, and Merle and Jess started to giggle.

'Shut up,' I said, nudging each of them. I didn't want Summers to get suspicious. Beverly limped her way to the changing room.

I suppose I should have felt guilty, or sorry for her, but my only thought was that now I was certain of being liked by Carol. She walked beside me as we left the playground. She even put her arm around my waist for a moment. I'd proved myself. I was at least as good as her and Jess and Merle. I knew I'd be included in everything from that moment on. The combination of this and the Little Angel column had made me a person to be reckoned with. It occurred to me that Beverly might tell Patience, but I no longer cared. Patience had made me look an idiot in front of hundreds of thousands of newspaper readers. What did it matter if we never spoke to each other again? And Beverly, she was just a sap. She deserved everything she got.

But then, as we sat in the classroom listening to each other stumbling over French conversation, I became more and more aware of the empty space beside me. Beverly had probably been sent home. Maybe she'd had to go to hospital. I remembered the look that she'd given me as she was falling. The glimmer of tears had been in her eyes. I pushed the memory away, and instead I smiled across at Carol, who smiled back, and then at Jess, who whispered, '*Aimez-vous* Beverly? *Elle est un cochon*,' and then began to giggle again. All four of us giggled; we got to the stage where we couldn't stop ourselves. It was infectious, and suddenly, the rest of the class picked it up too. '*Aimez-vous* Beverly? *Elle est un cochon*,' went round and round the class.

*

Carol had a group of hangers-on, who tried to get her attention with sweets and magazines. I'm not sure why we all found her so captivating. Perhaps it was because she favoured so few with her smiles, and remained so aloof and contemptuous. Or maybe it was because she was clever and seemed at least a little dangerous. She was certainly beautiful. She was slim and tall and she wore the most wonderful clothes out of school. I didn't just want to be like Carol, I actually wanted to be her. My only outstanding feature was being the daughter of a famous singer, but few people under forty had even heard of her. Carol's dad was a well-known actor. He was on television all the time and his picture was often in the Sunday papers. Everyone wanted an invite to Carol's house. Everybody wanted to get a glimpse of her dad.

So when she asked me round that afternoon, I was disappointed to discover that Carol lived in a very ordinary block of flats a short bus ride from our school. There wasn't even a porter, just an entryphone system. As we took the lift to the fourth floor, she said, 'Don't expect to see my dad. He and my mum are divorced. He hasn't lived with us in years.'

'Ditto,' I said, pleased to think that we had so much in common.

'If you tell anyone that, you're dead. I really mean it, OK?'

'OK,' I said. 'I won't tell, I promise.' Carol's secrecy and the way she kept herself so apart from the rest of us was starting to make sense. We'd all assumed she had this brilliant life, meeting famous people every minute. It was an image she obviously wanted to keep.

'I only see him once or twice a year. My mum's married to someone else now. His name's Bob and I don't really get on with him, he's a miserable git. Don't worry, though, he won't be home. He doesn't get in till six.'

I was pleased that Carol was confiding in me. You only tell the important things to people you really trust. She wouldn't have risked telling me if she'd thought we might fall out. I was definitely a friend of hers now, maybe even her best friend. I couldn't help smiling.

Carol's mum was attractive and young-looking. She gave me freshly squeezed orange juice to drink.

'You know the Little Angel bit that you read in the paper the other day?' said Carol.

Her mother laughed and said, 'That Angel could be you, I'm telling you.'

'If you really want to know, it's Grace. Patience Oswald, the person who writes that stuff, is her gran.'

I concentrated hard on my orange juice. 'It isn't really me. It's just that she put in some of the stuff that happened to me.'

Mrs Goodman laughed again and said, 'She's clever then, your gran. Really, Angel's every girl over the age of eleven. You're all stroppy little monsters, I don't know how we stand any of you.'

'Thanks a lot,' said Carol. 'Can we watch telly?'

'For half an hour or so. Then Bob will be home. You know he always likes to see the *News*.'

'Why do we always have to do what he wants, all the time?' Carol asked. Her mother didn't answer.

Carol and I watched a bit of TV while her mum sat out on their balcony, but mostly we talked. I told her some of the things that Jess had said to me about Merle.

'What does she say about me?'

I looked down. 'Nothing much.'

'Go on, tell me.'

So I did repeat some of the stuff. And it turned out just as I'd thought – most of what she said wasn't even true. Maybe I shouldn't have said anything, but I wanted Carol to like me, not her.

'She's a laugh though,' said Carol at the end of it.

I nodded, but then I said, 'She shouldn't lie about people, though.'

Carol just shrugged. 'She's a laugh,' she repeated. 'You know, you're OK too. You were so funny today when you got Beverly. She's such a pain. Why doesn't she get herself some decent clothes? And her voice. Have you noticed that she shouts all the time?'

'She honks,' I said. 'Beverly *est un cochon.*' We couldn't stop laughing.

Carol's mother came back in then. 'Bob will be home in a minute,' she said, and I knew I was being told to make myself scarce.

Carol showed me to the door. 'I just can't believe that Beverly's your cousin. You're so different.'

'I know, it's weird,' I said and I made a honking sound, holding my nose. Carol started laughing again and I joined in, pleased that I could keep her amused.

But as I walked home, I kept on seeing Beverly's sad face, even though I continued to tell myself that she deserved it and that I didn't care.

Seventeen

Patience was waiting in the hall again when I got home. It was becoming a habit. She looked unhappy, I thought; she'd looked that way ever since I'd found out about Little Angel.

'Hi,' I said, as I came through the door. This was the first time I'd spoken to her in three days. She looked ecstatic, but all she said was a cautious 'Hello' in return.

She followed me upstairs. This time, I let her into my room. She stood there like a cushion that's had some of its stuffing knocked out.

'I am sorry, Grace,' she said. 'You know, I do things without thinking. I don't consider the consequences. I'm really sorry you got hurt.'

'I wasn't hurt,' I said coolly. I didn't want her to know how much she'd upset me. It was to do with pride more than anything.

'I'm sorry, darling. I wouldn't have hurt you for the world. It was a silly thing to do. The paper asked me if I knew anyone who could write some humorous pieces about a teenage girl. I thought the money would come in handy so I decided to do it myself. Only I couldn't think what to write. And then you came and I put in some of the things that you said and I made up the rest. I didn't think you'd mind. I suppose I didn't think you'd see it.'

'It was a terrible thing to do,' I said, although in fact I'd started to be grateful for Little Angel; it had made me famous, in a way, and had got me some admiring friends. I had no intention of telling Patience this though; there was no way I was going to encourage her.

'I'm sorry,' Gran repeated. 'Forgive me?'

'Did Beverly know you were doing it?'

'No, I didn't say a word to her.'

'Are you going to write any more Little Angel pieces?'

'No,' she said humbly.

'OK then,' I told her, 'I forgive you.'

I don't think anyone had ever apologized to me before. I can't remember Mum doing so, but then I'd seen so little of her that there probably hadn't been much opportunity for her to make mistakes. I felt very important and quite happy, in a way; at least Patience had said sorry to me as if my feelings mattered.

Up in my room, I thought about Carol and the way she'd allowed me to go home with her. It was such a relief that she liked me. I'd been so scared that I'd have to do everything on my own, or with Beverly for company.

The more I knew Bev, the more ashamed of her I felt. Patience was an embarrassment too, but it didn't matter so much with her because she was a grown-up, and grown-ups nearly always looked stupid, you came to expect it of them. But Beverly should have known better. When you're black, you have to have certain standards or everyone thinks you're hopeless. They don't think your being useless is just one of those things, a sort of unlucky accident, they think you're useless because of your colour, and it reflects on all the other black people you know. Jess, Merle and Carol always looked right. They acted proud. They never let anyone get away with thinking they were no good. Beverly let people think that about her all the time. She almost seemed to revel in it.

Later that evening, there was a ring at the door. Patience answered it. The sound of Beverly's honking drifted up the staircase. I froze. I crept downstairs and listened, scared that she'd tell Gran what had happened in basketball that day. I knew that if Gran found out, she'd never forgive me. She'd never forgive anyone that hurt her favourite grandchild.

But Beverly and Patience didn't seem to be talking about me at all. They were having yet another riveting discussion about computer games. I opened the door and peeped inside. They were getting a new one out of a box and reading the instructions for loading it. 'You can't play this out quickly,' Bev shouted. 'It'll take us at least a couple of hours.'

'That's fine by me,' Patience said, and they both sat down in front of the computer.

'I saw a frog you haven't got yesterday,' Beverly

told her. 'It was made of fur fabric and it was sitting up with its legs crossed.'

'Like Jeremy Fisher?'

'Sort of, but not as lifelike, more cartoonish.'

I envied the way Beverly talked so easily to Patience. She didn't seem awkward, or get cross. And she knew how to tell the difference between every single one of Gran's frogs which was more than I could ever do.

I hung around outside the door for a while longer, just in case Beverly decided to tell Gran any tales, but they seemed to be totally engrossed in the game, so in the end, I left them to it and went back upstairs.

As soon as I reached my room, my knees began to shake. I realized how scared I'd been that Beverly would tell, just when Patience and I had resumed diplomatic relations. I didn't want Patience to be angry with me or to think I wasn't worth knowing any more. It was worrying me so much. And yet, at the same time, that afternoon with Carol, I'd been treated like one of the gang, someone important, not an outsider. And that mattered to me more than anything, I think.

So I waited for Beverly on the landing, and when she came upstairs to use the bathroom, I pounced.

She jumped and said, 'What do you want?' in a scared sort of way.

It was so simple to frighten her, it was hard not to enjoy it. 'Come in here,' I told her, and I pulled her into my room. I pushed her face into the duvet and held her head so she couldn't move it. 'If you tell anyone about today, you're dead, OK?' I said, using the same words Carol had used on me earlier when we'd been talking about her dad. I kept holding down Beverly's face. She started to make little choking sounds. I thought she was just pretending, but the sounds got worse, so I let her up again. She began to cough and splutter. For a moment, I was scared. She was so easy to hurt. You could kill people doing that to them. What if I'd really hurt her?

But then I remembered it was just Beverly, and she was pretty well indestructible, she just made a big fuss about everything. She liked the attention. She was a sad person. 'Go on, get out of my sight,' I told her, and she ran off into the bathroom, half crying.

I knew she wouldn't tell anyone then. She was such a coward. But even though I believed I was safe, I still felt a bit worried, so I followed her downstairs and sat with her and Gran for the rest of the evening, warning Bev with my eyes to remember not to tell.

I liked the way I could make her do whatever I wanted. It was amazing that you could tell somebody you'd kill them and have them believe you. It was funny and weird, and almost scary. I couldn't wait till tomorrow. Carol and Merle and Jess would laugh like crazy when they heard what I'd done to Bev with the duvet.

Yet I couldn't sleep that night. I worried that someone would find me out. And I worried too that my friends would soon get tired of me and that

I'd be all on my own, the way that Bev was. I tried to shut it all out by thinking of the G family. I closed my eyes and imagined them into my life, but for once, it didn't really work. Every time I conjured them up, they just seemed to ignore me. Griselda was putting on make-up in her bedroom. I went to share it with her, but she pushed me away. Gilbert and Gerry were having a game of cards in the living room, but although I sat myself between the pair of them, they never once dealt me into the game.

Eighteen

At the bottom of the playground, near the playing fields, there was a small wood with a trickle of water running through it that was meant to be a stream. It didn't belong to the school, so we weren't meant to be there, but Merle, Jess, Carol and I never bothered much about rules. It was fun to spend lunchtimes there, knowing no teachers would see us and trying to avoid the dampest patches on the grass. I'd just finished telling them about Beverly and the duvet. They were impressed. They could hardly believe I'd done it. Then Jess tossed a pebble. It was supposed to fall in the water, but instead it flew right over it and landed on the other side. Jess looked so surprised that we all started laughing. Then Carol stood up and said, 'There's Bev now, mooching along the edge of the playground.'

We all turned to look, but only Carol seemed to be able to see her.

'Are you sure she's there?' asked Jess, shielding her eyes against the sun.

'Yeah, she's there. It's like she's hiding.'

I stood up too, in order to get a glimpse of her. For a moment or two there was nothing, and then a piece of Beverly's blue anorak came into view.

'She is there,' I said. 'Keep looking towards the chestnut tree. She's close to that.'

'I can see her,' said Merle. 'Is she spying on us or what?'

'Of course she is,' I said. 'It's just the kind of creepy thing she would do.' I didn't really think that, but I was enjoying the role of chief Beverly-hater.

'She does give me the creeps,' said Merle. 'I can't stand it when she keeps looking at us all the time.'

'She wants to be one of us,' said Carol astutely.

'Well, she can't,' said Jess. 'She's useless. How could she be one of us?'

I started laughing again then. We all did. Then Carol said, 'We ought to show her that she isn't one of us.'

'She can't hold a proper conversation, she has to shout all the time,' said Merle.

'What gets me is the way she wears those awful clothes,' said Jess.

'Her hair hasn't been cut in years,' I said, 'it's all natty and she doesn't use a decent hair conditioner, you can tell. I hate it when people don't get their hair done right. If you get the cheap conditioners, you smell like a Bounty bar, it's the coconut oil.'

'Go and get her,' said Carol.

'How?' asked Merle. She was always the practical one.

'Drag her here if you have to,' said Carol.

I decided to let Merle and Jess fetch her. I wanted to wait with Carol, but as I continued to stand there, she said, 'You've got to go too.'

'Why?'

'Because you have, right?'

I remained where I was for a moment, but Carol's forceful gaze made me follow the others back to the playing field, where Beverly was lurking.

I watched from a distance as the others acted out a kind of dumb show. Beverly was obviously refusing to come; she stood there, poised, as if she might run away at any moment. Merle faced her stridently while Jess began to pull her by the arm. There was a struggle. Then Merle held her too and they both began to propel her to the wood where Carol was waiting. I followed slowly. It didn't really seem right, four against one. And Beverly was one of us; her skin was the same deep shade.

I'm not really sure what happened next. Someone – Jess, I think, though it might have been Carol – said that Beverly was letting everyone down and ought to be punished for it. I remember feeling a surge of excitement, the kind you get when you think you're about to get a goal in a match or win a prize in a lucky draw. And then Carol shouted, 'Get her!' and we all started chucking things at her: mud from the water's edge, and small, sharp stones. She was yelping and crying at the same time, and I despised her for not standing up to us, for letting us do it to her. Her anorak was soaked; there were blue-green stains across the front of it. And her cheek was bleeding where it had been scratched by one of the stones.

Then suddenly, she saw a gap between Jess and

Merle and she charged through it. They began to run after her, but I shouted, 'Let her go, she's had enough,' and to my surprise they stopped and let her get away.

'What you do that for?' Carol asked.

'It's all right for you, she isn't related to you, I'll have my gran giving me the third degree all night,' I said.

'Anyway, it's time to go in,' said Merle, and we hurried back into school through a gap in the fence.

Beverly didn't turn up for the afternoon register. In one way, I was relieved; people would have asked questions if she'd arrived with her clothes all muddy and her face scratched. But then I began to worry again. What if we'd really hurt her? I was starting to think about what might happen to us if anyone realized what we'd done. And I also felt mean, I couldn't seem to stop myself, and it was such a horrible feeling that I could hardly stand it. So instead I convinced myself that it hadn't been as bad as all that, just a bit of fun; Bev was so pathetic that things always looked worse than they were with her. And I told myself again that anyone as beyond hope as Beverly was bound to get teased, people simply couldn't help themselves. I settled down to enjoy the English TV programme we were watching with Mrs Power, and as the story unfolded, I pushed the afternoon's events to the back of my mind until they hardly troubled me.

*

I went round to Merle's again after school. Her mother had left some packets of microwave popcorn, the stuff that grows in the packet when you turn the power on and then starts popping till it's ready. Merle was lucky to have a microwave. Patience thought she was so up to date with everything, but she didn't have much that was really useful. Just a few million frogs and a rather stupid cat.

Somehow, I couldn't get Patience out of my head that afternoon. I kept thinking about how much she'd hate me if she knew about Bev. She wouldn't understand that it isn't possible to like people just because they're family. She wouldn't understand that at all.

Merle was flicking through a magazine. She looked up and said, 'Do you think Bev's all right?'

I shrugged, like I didn't care.

'Perhaps we shouldn't have done it,' she said.

'She deserved it, she got what was coming to her,' I answered, quoting Carol, but inside I was starting to worry again.

'It's silly, but sometimes I feel a bit guilty about her,' Merle answered. 'I mean, I know how awful she is, and I don't want to be her friend or anything like that, but maybe we should leave her alone sometimes.'

'She'll be OK,' I said. 'Anyway, she's got to learn.'

'Learn what?' asked Merle.

'Oh, you know,' I said. I wasn't really sure, I just

wanted Merle to be impressed with me and to see how tough I was.

But then Merle said, 'I wish Carol didn't have to be so hard all the time. Sometimes I wish I had different friends. I don't mean you.' She suddenly looked scared. 'You won't tell Carol I said that, will you? She wouldn't like it at all.'

I shook my head. Sometimes I wished I had different friends too, even though Carol was the best at everything and was the person I most wanted to be like.

When I got home that evening, Patience was on the phone. I listened for a moment. It was Uncle James. My breathing went haywire for a second or two – had Beverly told him what had happened? Patience halted the conversation and turned to me and said, 'Bev hasn't come home, and she was meant to get tea for her mum. It's not like her. Do you know where she could have gone?'

I shook my head.

Patience went back to the phone again. 'She says she doesn't know. Don't worry, I expect she's lost track of the time, you know what a dreamer she is. Or maybe she forgot about tea and is on her way here . . .'

I didn't stop to listen to any more; I ran up into the bathroom and locked the door. I put down the lid of the toilet seat and sat there, trying to stop my knees from shaking. They were going to find out what I'd done, they were bound to . . . Maybe

Beverly was lying bleeding somewhere from her wounds. Perhaps she was dying even . . . I thought about the duvet again. That would come out too, if she was badly hurt. Doing that to people was a criminal offence, you could go to prison for it. I imagined the newspaper headline: *Opera singer's daughter murders cousin in cold blood*. Well, it hadn't been cold blood, not really, and she might not be dead; it was important to keep calm and not to jump to conclusions.

But even as I thought that, horrible images of dead and mangled people kept coming into my head. I imagined my mother flying back to Britain for the trial, full of sorrow and disappointment in me. And Patience would be sitting sadly in the public gallery, vivid in her orange jacket with a pink and yellow scarf and everyone would say, that's the child's grandmother, no wonder she turned out to be a murderer, her relatives have got such awful taste . . .

Nineteen

It was gone nine o'clock and Beverly still hadn't come home. Patience kept saying, 'Are you sure you don't know what could have happened to her?' and I kept saying, 'I told you, I don't have any idea,' which added lying to my list of sins.

I was getting more scared by the minute. The mangled Beverly pictures were strong in my mind now, and they wouldn't go away. I wished that I'd been kinder to her. I wished I'd tried to like her just a bit.

Patience sat by the phone, waiting for news. She looked utterly miserable. 'It's not like her,' she said to me over and over again. 'I think something must have happened. James has called the police.'

It was over, then. The police would find out what I did for sure. I began to cry, great heaving, noisy sobs that shook my whole body.

Patience misunderstood. She took me in her arms and said, 'Don't worry, we'll find her, I'm sure we will. It's all right, darling.'

I wanted her to hold me and call me darling for ever. But I knew that because of what I'd done to Beverly, she'd probably disown me. I sat beside her, wishing I could tell her all about it, but scared of what would happen if I did.

'There,' she said, 'you just take it easy. Everything's going to be all right.'

It wasn't all right though – she was comforting me, even though it was all my fault.

At half-past nine, there was another phone call. Beverly had come home. She was safe.

I knew what grown-ups were like. They'd question her endlessly about why she'd gone. Would my death threat be enough to keep her quiet or would she tell? I sat in the living room shaking with the fear of yet another phone call – one that would tell Patience what I'd done. At ten o'clock I went up to bed, but I hardly slept at all that night.

Next morning, I got up very early. There didn't seem to be any sense in remaining in bed, tossing and turning. I knew Patience wouldn't be up, so I put on my tracksuit bottoms and hooded top and slipped out for a run.

I wasn't allowed to go out without asking, but I really didn't care. I wanted some time to think. When you're on edge, and the adrenalin's going, running is the best thing in the world. It stops the restlessness, calms you down. I took my usual route, round by the little post office at the end of the street and then towards the park. I knew I had to stay on the street; Patience would have a fit if I went inside the park gates. In that sense, she was very like my mother, careful of me and worried about anything that could do me harm. 'You've got to be so street-wise these days, Grace,' she'd say, shaking her head slowly. I knew she was right – I watched the news too.

The mangled Beverly pictures flashed into my mind again and I thought some more about last night. But slowly, the fear began to fade and I began to feel angry with Beverly for all the worry that she'd caused. What we'd done hadn't been so very bad. It was typical of her to hype it up and run away. She was so gutless. A braver person would have faced it out.

I felt a lot happier. It hadn't really been my fault anyway. The others had done most of it, and I had stopped them throwing stones when it had looked like going too far. Besides, you had to be able to take a bit of teasing. If you couldn't, you might as well lay down and die.

I paused for a moment and watched a girl two or three years older than me being dragged into the park by a huge wheaten terrier. I'd always wanted a dog, but with all the travelling Mum and I had done, it had been impossible. If only she'd come back to Britain for good. Living with Patience had made me realize how tired I was of being on the move. I wanted a permanent home, with my friends always round me, and a cosy fireside where I could sit with my faithful hound.

Patience was up by the time I got back.

'You should have left a note for me. I was worried half to death. After last night, I'd have thought you'd have realized that.'

'Sorry,' I said.

Patience continued to look cross and said, 'There was another phone call from James while you were out.'

My mouth went dry. Beverly must have told. I looked down at the floor.

'Beverly won't go to school. She says she hates it and she never wants to go back.'

Patience paused here, obviously waiting for me to say something. I remained silent. 'Grace, do you know anything about this?' she added, after a while.

I shook my head.

'Are the other kids giving her a hard time? I know she got bullied in junior school, and a lot of the same crowd are in her new class.'

'Well, they don't like her much, but I wouldn't say she was being bullied,' I answered, relieved that Patience wasn't imagining it was anything to do with me.

'How would you describe it?'

'Look, don't go on at me. If Beverly's having a bad time, it isn't down to me. Leave me out of it, OK?'

Patience looked concerned. 'Grace, are you being bullied too? It isn't easy for African-Caribbean children, they're often made to feel outsiders.'

'No, nothing like that's going on.' As soon as I'd said it, I knew I'd made a mistake. It would have been so much easier if I'd given the impression that Beverly was being bullied by white kids because she was black. The truth was more complicated than that, but in a way, it was to do with colour; it was to do with the embarrassment that Beverly made us feel by being less cool than we were. If she'd been a white kid, we would have left her alone. It was because she was one of us and yet different from us. It was because she always let us down by behaving stupidly. Patience would never understand though. She'd never see the way it was.

'Grace, if you know anything at all about what's going on, please tell me. Bev's so unhappy.'

'I expect she's worried about her school work. She's not very good at it and some of the teachers give her a bad time.'

'Which teachers?'

'You need to ask her, not me.' It was a bad move, I realized that as soon as I said it. Beverly wouldn't last under interrogation. She was too weak. 'Well, maybe you shouldn't worry her at the moment with a lot of questions,' I added.

Patience gave me one of her beaming smiles. She thought I understood Beverly, and cared about her. Once again, she thought I was concerned.

'I have to get changed. I'll be late for school,' I said, and I bounded up the stairs, knowing that if I started to feel any more guilty I might blurt out the truth.

When I came back down again, Patience was dressed too. She was wearing a sweatshirt with a huge frog sitting on a lily pad printed on the front. She smiled at me and said, 'I thought I'd walk in with you, talk to Mary, see if she's got any ideas about what's going on.'

'I'm in a hurry. I'm late. I thought I might jog in this morning.'

'No, you've already had a run. You'll wear yourself out.'

'Exercise is good for you.'

Patience shook her head slowly. 'Too much and you drop down dead, you hear it all the time, all these runners with heart failure. Everything in moderation.'

Moderation. Patience didn't know the meaning of the word. 'I'm going to try to meet the others. They go past the High Street in about ten minutes. I want to catch them.'

'You'll see them in school. Come on, we'll go together.'

'Are you going to wear a jacket?' I asked hopefully.

'No, the weather's warm. It's a nice spring day.'

'It's cold out, much colder than it looks. I wished I'd put on something warmer when I went out, and I wasn't just walking, I was running.'

'I'll be fine,' Patience said with a warm smile. 'You know, you're such a good girl, always worrying about whether I'll be too hot or too cold. But I've got nice warm blood, I don't catch chills. I'm a very healthy person.'

I realized there was no more point in arguing. I followed Patience slowly out of the house.

We arrived at school just as the bell was about to ring, so everybody was assembled in the playground.

I edged away from Patience, trying to give the impression that we were standing beside one another by chance, but I doubt if anyone was fooled. They stared at us and nudged one another, big grins on their faces. It wasn't just the sweatshirt. Patience was wearing the silver ankle boots again.

'I'll just go up to see Mary. Come straight home from school, you hear? I don't want any worry about you as well today.'

I muttered something without moving my lips in case anybody thought I actually talked to this strange woman. Up ahead, I saw Merle, Jess and Carol. They were leaning against the wall, looking completely cool and unworried. My news was going to change all that. I pushed my way through the various groups and ended up beside them. 'Hi,' they said, in chorus.

'We have to talk,' I told them. 'Something's happened. It's an emergency.'

I began to tell them about the previous night and the way that Beverly had refused to go into school that morning. Carol just shrugged. 'No sweat, if she does decide to tell anyone, it's her word against ours. You're her cousin. No one will think you could be involved. They won't believe her story.'

'They might,' I said, thinking of Carol's reputation for giving smaller kids grief, and the way I'd behaved with Beverly when I'd been at her house.

'Trust me,' said Carol.

Whenever people say 'Trust me', I know I have something to worry about. 'Listen, Carol,' I said to her, but she turned her back on me and went on talking to Jess.

I tried again. 'Listen, you don't understand. Bev's my cousin, I'll get into trouble with my whole family. It's all right for you, this is just a school thing, but for me, it's a home thing too.'

Carol turned to me again and looked bored. 'What do you want me to do about it then?' she asked, in a challenging tone.

'I don't know. I just know we have to do something.'

'The trouble with you, Grace, is that you're almost as sad as your cousin,' replied Carol. 'You always need someone else to do your thinking for you. You don't have any ideas of your own.'

'That's not true. What about basketball? What about the death threat?'

'I mean real ideas. Things to get you out of trouble, not just into it.'

'So how do you get us out of trouble then?' I demanded crossly.

'I don't. You see, I don't mind trouble all that much, I'm not scared of it, so I don't need to try to avoid it all the time.'

'I'm not scared of trouble,' I said, though inside I knew I was very scared of it. 'It's just sensible though, not to get into more than you can help. Why don't we lay off her for a bit? Then she'll come back to school and everything will be all right.'

Carol and Jess started laughing. Merle just looked uncomfortable. Carol said, 'And if she isn't here, how's she going to know we're laying off her then?'

They'd spotted the deliberate mistake. 'I know,' I said, 'I just meant . . .' Only I didn't know what I meant any more.

The bell went then and we all straggled inside. I couldn't concentrate on lessons that morning, I was too concerned about Gran's visit to Mrs Harcourt and whether or not Beverly had started to tell the grown-ups all the things I'd done. At dinner time, I sat on my own. Carol was treating me like I had a contagious disease and Merle and Jess were following her lead. I kept my eyes on my plate and tried not to mind.

Just before afternoon school, Beverly walked through the dining room. I almost went up to her to ask what was happening and why she'd come back, but I knew she had no reason to tell me – quite the reverse.

At registration, she took her normal place beside me. We were working on a map of somewhere or other. She was rubbing holes in the paper as usual. I was busy wondering what she'd said to people, so I lost concentration and started rolling my pencil about on the desk. Suddenly I dropped it and it landed by her feet. I moved towards her to pick it up and she flinched as if she thought I was going to hit her. I stared at her, wondering how she could possibly be that scared of someone like me. I realized then how she saw me. I was a kind of monster to her.

Halfway through the last lesson, Carol passed me

a note. It said, *If you want to stick with us, make sure you meet us by the bins after school. Bring Beverly.*

I scribbled hastily, *Why? What for?* and folded the message and passed it across.

Because I say so, came the reply.

Suddenly, it didn't seem good enough. Why did I always end up jumping whenever Carol told me to? The answer came to me quickly – it was because I wanted to fit in. I wanted to be her friend. I thought back to the lonely dinner time I'd had, sitting at a table by myself in the school canteen and then standing by the wall on my own afterwards. I thought of spending weeks, months, even years like that. It was impossible. I didn't want Beverly's life. It was too depressing.

I have to go to the doctor tonight, I scrawled on another scrap of paper. I needed to buy some time.

Tomorrow then, Carol replied. *I'm working on something big.*

I tried to imagine what it could be, but Carol was right, I was short on ideas. Something nasty, anyway.

After school, I was torn between hurrying home to know the worst and dawdling to hold off whatever grief might be waiting for me. But as I left the school building, I saw that Carol and the others were watching, so I knew I'd have to go straight home to make the doctor's appointment seem convincing.

Patience wasn't waiting for me, which seemed a good sign. She was in the living room, printing out an article.

'Not Little Angel, I hope,' I said to her.

She shook her head. 'I told you, I won't do any more of them. Mind you, it is costing me. They liked them you know. They said they wanted one a week. They even talked about a book.'

'*Quel dommage!*' I said. The last lesson had been French. Then I asked as casually as I could, 'How was it with Contrary Mary?'

Patience grinned. 'Is that what you all call her?'

'It's what *I* call her.'

'She's no wiser than we are. Bev hasn't said anything to the staff.'

I was relieved to hear it, but I said nothing.

'Did Beverly go in this afternoon?'

I nodded.

'Good. James said he thought he could persuade her.'

I wondered how he'd managed it. He'd probably told poor old Bev that she ought to try to be more like me.

'How did she seem?' asked Patience.

'Much the same as usual,' I answered, and then I remembered the way my pencil had rolled by her chair and how she'd looked when I'd tried to fetch it. I was starting to feel quite sorry for her. What with the pencil, and sitting in the canteen at dinner time, I'd begun to imagine what life was like for her. She was never included in anything. And then there was her home life too. Her mum was ill, and Uncle James didn't seem to think much of her, and he was her own father. No wonder she didn't stand up for herself. And then finally I remembered Carol's note, and the big thing she'd said she was working on and I knew that I didn't want to be part of it any more. But what could I do? As I went to bed that night, I felt weighed down with the awfulness of everything. I wished I'd never come to live with Patience. I wished I'd stayed with Mum.

Twenty

Early next morning, Patience came into the bathroom before I'd finished. I hadn't bothered to lock the door because she was seldom up before eight fifteen, so she caught me peering into the mirror, trying to see myself as Beverly saw me.

'Don't tell me,' she said. 'Spots.'

'I've never had a spot in my life,' I told her crossly.

'All kids get spots. It's nothing to be embarrassed about.'

I had a terrible feeling that she was warming up to another Little Angel story. 'You're not thinking of writing this, are you?' I said.

Patience looked pained. 'I told you I wouldn't.' Then, after a pause, she added wistfully, 'It is a pity though . . .'

'*Patience!*'

'Just kidding,' she said. 'Had you there, didn't I?' and we both began to laugh.

That was the thing about Patience: she was irritating and childish sometimes, but she was fun to be with. I don't think I was really able to laugh before I came to live with her. I don't mean that Mum didn't have a sense of humour, it's just that she was always so busy. Either she actually was somewhere else or she was so wrapped up in planning the next performance that she might as well have been. Patience was dependable, she was always there. And she was always ready for fun, there was little solemnity around her. Even though she was old, Patience was the most alive person I knew.

As she went out of the bathroom, I turned back to the mirror again. What did Patience see when she looked at me? Right now, she seemed to like me a lot, but once she found out about Beverly, things would be different. The laughter faded. Maybe I could refuse to go to school the way that Beverly had done. It was hard to see any other way out of the mess I'd got myself into.

I did go though, in the end. There would have been too many questions otherwise. And I didn't want Patience jumping to any conclusions.

Carol was waiting for me as I arrived at school. 'Don't forget, meet me by the shed after school, and make sure Bev comes with you.'

'Why? What are you going to do?' I asked.

Carol tapped her nose to signal that it was for her to know and for me to find out. It was an annoying gesture. As if she sensed that I was feeling less than thrilled with her, she tucked her arm into mine and said, 'You can come home with me again after, if you want.'

'Thanks,' I said, forgetting, for a moment, to be cross.

Merle and Jess came up then. 'She says she'll meet us, and she's going to bring Bev,' Carol told them.

I didn't remember saying anything like that, but Jess gave me a huge smile. Merle looked a bit worried, but at the same time, she seemed pleased to see me. I grinned back at them, too relieved that hostilities had been suspended to worry about that afternoon. Patience kept telling me I worried too much. 'You have to try to live for the moment,' she told me constantly. Just then, it seemed like good advice.

Have you ever noticed that whenever there's something you don't want to happen, time rushes by? Afternoon school ended so quickly that I thought there must have been something wrong with the clock. And of course, adopting Gran's philosophy had meant that I hadn't made any plans either for getting Bev to the shed, or explaining why I hadn't done it. I knew that I was in deep trouble.

Beverly's chair scraped across the floor as she stood up just after the rest of us. I caught her sleeve and tugged her downwards. She gave me her really scared look, which made me want to feed her to Carol and the others there and then. Instead though, I whispered, 'They're going to be waiting for you. Don't go out there.' I don't know which of us was more surprised, her or me. Until that moment, I hadn't thought I'd go against Carol and the rest.

Bev's surprised expression quickly turned to one of suspicion.

'I'm telling you the truth,' I said.

But she didn't trust me. 'Let me go,' she said.

Mrs Power was still in the classroom. She turned to look at us. 'What's going on?' she said.

'Nothing,' we both answered together.

'Then hurry up and get your things together. Haven't you got homes to go to?'

I swept my belongings into my bag and hurried after Beverly, who had already reached the door.

'I'm serious, Bev, don't go out there.'

'Leave me alone,' she said, pulling away from me.

'Listen, I've got an idea. Let's wait for Mrs Power. We'll leave with her.'

'What do you mean?'

'You heard. Just stick with me.'

Mrs Power came outside and locked the classroom door. I attached myself to her, offering to carry her books. Beverly followed us. As we passed the shed, I couldn't help gloating. Carol, Jess and Merle were staring at us. There was a mixture of disbelief, anger and fear on their faces. Beverly edged as close to Mrs Power as she could. I saw that at last she believed me. She threw me a look of surprised gratitude. I looked away, embarrassed.

I was half afraid that Carol and the rest would be waiting for us when we finally left Mrs Power at the High Street, but there was no sign of them. We walked along awkwardly, not sure what to say to one another. Then Beverly said, 'I thought I'd go to see Patience tonight. Can I go back with you?'

I couldn't really say no, so I just nodded.

'Why did you warn me?' Beverly asked.

'I don't really know,' I answered.

'Thanks anyway,' she said.

'That's OK,' I replied, still embarrassed. She probably thought we were friends now, but we weren't, it was impossible.

'They'll be angry with you.'

I knew she meant Carol and the others. I shrugged. Then I said, 'I don't think Merle will be, I think she'll be relieved.'

Beverly nodded. 'She's nicer than the others. She's weak though. She goes along with them just because it's easier.'

It seemed funny for Beverly to be describing one of us as weak. It was how we always thought of her. Then I remembered that there probably wasn't any 'we' any more. After the way I'd failed to deliver Beverly, I'd be on my own.

It was such a frightening thought that I nearly burst into tears right there and then. I should have let Beverly sort out her own problems. I shouldn't have interfered.

'I nearly stopped going to school,' Beverly suddenly confided.

'I know,' I answered abruptly, feeling cross with her again.

We fell silent then, and walked the rest of the way without further conversation.

Patience was out when we arrived. She'd left me a note to say she'd forgotten that she had an interview to do that afternoon and that I was to go on to Beverly's house; it had been fixed with Uncle James. I gave Beverly the bad news.

'OK,' she said. 'We'd better go then.'

It seemed silly to be walking along the street together in silence, so in the end I said, 'Did you understand the maths homework?' Not because I particularly wanted to know but because it was something to say.

'I never understand,' answered Beverly. 'Dad says I've got a brain the size of a pea.'

'I think your dad's mean,' I told her.

'No, he's just truthful. I'm not all that clever. You know I'm not. It's why you don't like me either.'

'Well, it isn't just that,' I answered, unable, for some reason, to be tactful.

'What else is it then?'

'I don't know,' I said.

'Yes you do. Go on, tell me. I'd like to know.'

'Well, I suppose it's your clothes. And you don't stick up for yourself, you just take everything people dish out to you.'

'So do you,' Beverly replied.

'But I'm . . .' I struggled to think of the difference between us. 'I don't know, exactly. I just know how to behave. But you don't really.'

There was a pause while Beverly digested this. 'You say the right thing. I don't.' It was a statement rather than a question.

'I dress right and do the right thing in school and at home. You don't.'

'Well, what do I get wrong?'

It was impossible to answer that. It was like trying

to describe the taste of water to someone who'd never drunk it before. Then I said, 'You don't fit in.'

'What would make me fit in?'

I wanted to say a personality transplant, but it seemed too cruel. 'People either fit or they don't. It's not a question of changing something.'

'Patience doesn't fit anything either, but people like her,' said Beverly. 'Look how many came to her party. And they all brought her presents.'

'Patience is a grown-up. Grown-ups don't have to behave like normal people. You know that.'

Beverly nodded slowly. 'I can't wait to be grown up,' she answered.

It's strange how people can say one simple thing and it gets to you more than anything they've ever said before. There was something really sad about Beverly wishing the next six or seven years away so that she could fit in somewhere. The funny thing was, much as I hated to admit it, I knew how she felt; I wanted to be grown up so much that it hurt. When you're a kid, you get pushed around. Your mother hardly notices you're there; you're minded by countless strangers and sent to a dozen different schools. Then you get parcelled off to live with a grandmother you haven't seen in years. I'd thought that Beverly and I were like chalk and cheese, but now I wasn't so sure.

We reached her house. Her mother was downstairs in the kitchen making a pot of tea. 'She's a lot better now,' Beverly whispered. I was relieved. One of the difficulties about being around Beverly was not knowing what to say about her mother.

Auntie Donna said how nice it was to see me and then packed Beverly and me upstairs to do our homework. As I went up to Beverly's little bedroom, I remembered the night I'd stayed with her and how hard it had been. But as she opened the door, I saw that it was different. 'You've got bunk beds,' I said.

'Mum got them for me. She said you might want to stay more if you had a bigger space to sleep.' Then she added, 'I told her you wouldn't, but she didn't really listen.'

I muttered something inaudible. She was right, bunk beds wouldn't make enough of a difference. I'd still have to share the room with Beverly.

We started taking our books out of our bags. Then Beverly said, 'What will happen tomorrow if they try to get me again?' and I knew that what she really wanted to know was if I would stand up for her again or beat up on her like the rest.

'I'm not sure,' I answered. It was hard for me to think what tomorrow would be like now that I'd crossed Carol.

'Will you get into trouble with them for helping me?'

I shrugged. I didn't want to talk about it.

'The last few weeks have been terrible,' said Beverly. 'I think sometimes I just wanted to curl up and die.'

I didn't want her to tell me this. It made me feel guilty. But she went on, 'You don't know what it's like, having everyone ignore you or be mean to you no matter what you do.'

'I do know,' I said, and I told her about that school I'd gone to where all the other kids had ignored me, day in, day out.

'It's a terrible feeling, isn't it?' Beverly said.

'I guess,' I answered.

'What do you think I should do?'

'How should I know? The trouble with you is, you keep letting people get away with it. You have to stand up for yourself, Bev, that's all there is to it.'

'They'll kill me,' she said.

I wasn't sure if she really believed they would or if it was just a way of talking. 'If you fight back, they'll lose interest, I promise you. It's because you let people walk all over you.'

'Did you fight back when you were being bullied at your old school?' she asked.

'No,' I answered, 'but then I knew I was only there for a term or two. If it happened again that's what I'd do.'

'You wouldn't. That day when they left you by yourself in the dining room, you just sat there.'

It was true, but I wasn't going to admit it. 'I was thinking of a plan. If they hadn't started being nice to me again, I would have fought back, believe me I would. No one messes with me.'

Beverly started laughing her deep, honking laugh. 'You're full of it,' she said.

'No, I would have,' I answered hotly.

'Oh yeah,' she said, 'who are you trying to kid?'

I was embarrassed to think that Beverly had seen through me. I squirmed under her laughter. And then it occurred to me. 'That's it!' I said.

'What do you mean?' she asked.

'That's how you do it, how you stand up for yourself. You make them look stupid. You show them you know what they're really like.'

'I don't understand.'

'What you did to me just now. You laughed at me. That's what you've got to do to them.'

Beverly opened her book and started fingering the pages but her mind was somewhere else. 'I can't,' she said. 'I'll mess it up. I'll forget what to say. I'll look stupid.'

'No, you won't. I know you can do it. Honestly. Just laugh at them, Bev. They'll hate it. They'll leave you alone, maybe not at once, but in the end they will. Nobody likes to be laughed at.'

'They'll hit me.'

'You have to keep laughing no matter what, even if they are hitting you,' I said, though I was no longer quite so sure of myself. Beverly did have a point.

'I can't,' she said.

'Oh, for goodness' sake! You really are hopeless, no wonder they keep picking on you. Have some pride.'

Beverly looked at me squarely. 'I do have pride,' she said.

'Then use it. You're not that bad. You helped your mum when she was ill. And you can laugh and fool around with Patience. I can't do that, not like you can. She likes you much better than she likes me.'

'She doesn't,' said Beverly, but I could tell that the idea had pleased her.

'You're a laugh, when you stop being scared. I'm never a laugh, not really.' And then I thought of the fun I had with Patience, and I was no longer quite so sure.

'Grace!' Beverly's mum was calling me. 'Time to go home. Patience is here.'

I was pleased to see her. I gave her a hug. I never give people hugs. She looked happy and surprised.

Then as we were walking home, Patience said, 'Grace, there's something I have to tell you.' I could see from her expression that it was serious. There was silence for a while, as if she couldn't bring herself to tell me. All sorts of horrors came into my mind. She'd found out what I'd been doing to Beverly. She was sending me away. Then at last Patience said, 'Your mum phoned this afternoon. She says she's missed you. She's flying here the week after next to see about taking you abroad again.'

I wrapped my fingers round my gran's arm. In some ways, I wanted to go back. I missed my mum. And it would get me out of trouble. I wouldn't have to bother dealing with Carol and the rest. I could just wave goodbye to them and get on a plane. But even as I thought it, I knew deep down that you don't get off the hook as easily as that.

And, as I held on to Patience, I knew I'd miss

living in just one place. I'd miss regular school in spite of all the problems. I'd even miss Marley, that fat old fleabag. And most of all, I'd miss laughing with my gran.

Twenty-one

Beverly called for me next morning. It wasn't that I felt OK about being seen with her. It was more that there was safety in numbers.

I'd spent most of the previous evening looking at Patience's back copies of *Maribeth* in the hope that I'd get some inspiration from the problem page on how to handle bullies. I'd wanted to ask Patience directly, but I hadn't dared to in the end – I was scared she'd guess why I wanted to know. There was a great deal on the subject, but most of it involved facing up to them at least a bit, and Beverly had already shown that she wasn't going to be much good at it.

I tried not to feel cross with her, but it was hard. If I wasn't careful I'd end up doing it all, and then they'd probably forget about Bev entirely and go after me instead. But reading all the stuff last night about kids who were dumped on by other kids to the point where they ran away or refused to go to school, or even sometimes killed themselves, had made me feel pretty embarrassed about myself and the way I'd been treating her.

In one issue, there was a school that had set up a kind of counselling service for kids who got bullied.

It was run by other kids who were taught how to help, and if you were being persecuted, you talked to these counsellors about the problems you were having. Then they helped you to talk to your attackers about what they were doing to you. I really liked that idea. I decided I wouldn't mind running something like that. I could see myself sorting out difficulties for everyone and being kind and understanding. I could imagine everybody wanting to see me and to be my friend. I'd known as I was reading about it, that I was born to deal with other people's problems, just like Patience really. I'd decided that once all this stuff with Beverly got sorted, I'd go to Mrs Harcourt with the idea of setting up a counselling service at our school.

Beverly dawdled beside me along the street. 'Dad says your mum's coming to visit,' she honked suddenly.

'Shush,' I said, 'I don't want the entire world to know.'

Beverly lowered her voice to a piercing whisper. 'Will you go back with her?'

I didn't want to tell Beverly my innermost thoughts, so instead I said, 'Have you decided what you're going to do if they start picking on you?'

Beverly began hopping from one leg to the other. 'I have to stand up for myself,' she said, but her voice, though loud, was faltering and her hands and knees were starting to shake. I didn't hold out much hope of a Beverly victory. I was definitely on the losing side. I turned round and walked back a few steps, not sure, for a moment, if I could bear to be around when all the embarrassing stuff started to happen. Carol would annihilate her, and me too, most probably. But after a moment, I faced forward again and tried not to mind the fact that Beverly was wearing her anorak and a pair of lace-topped ankle socks.

We went through the school gate together. Up ahead, Carol, Jess and Merle were waiting, along with half our year. 'It's smelly-belly Beverly,' Carol jeered, and the others took up the chant. Smelly-belly Beverly, smelly-belly Beverly, over and over. Round one to them, but at least they'd left me out of it. I pushed Beverly forward and waited. She had to stand up for herself now, she had no choice, it was either that or be at the receiving end of taunts and poundings for the rest of her days. She stood there in the midst of them, and I could see that she was steeling herself for the attack. She looked first at Carol, then at Merle, then at Jess. She tried to stare them out, but they were better at it by a long way and she was the one who lowered her eyes to the ground. Round two to the opposition as well, I thought. Bev's arms began to twitch. 'Now, Beverly,' I told her, 'do it now.'

She opened her mouth. I nudged her, willing her to tell them what she thought of them. But she just stood there, saying nothing, and everyone began to laugh.

'Cat got your tongue?' demanded Jess.

'She's so thick, she can't even talk,' said Carol.

'Useless,' said Merle, though her voice was barely a whisper.

'I –' squeaked Beverly.

'You what?' said Carol.

'You what, you what, you what,' said the others, in a deafening chorus.

Beverly started to run. She headed towards the playing fields. I began to follow her, and the others gave chase. Soon we were all tearing away from the school, even though the bell was ringing. 'Beverly!' I shouted, but I don't know if she heard. She just kept on running. 'Beverly!' I cried again, but my voice was lost in all the other voices.

Then, just as I thought the pack was going in for the kill, everything went quiet and they all stopped running. There didn't seem to be any reason for it. Everybody just stood there, brought to their senses suddenly.

'Let her go,' said Carol, in a disappointed tone. 'Mrs Power's coming.'

Beverly carried on running and disappeared into the bushes. Mrs Power shouted, 'Come inside at once. What on earth's going on?'

'Nothing,' said Jess. 'It was just a game we were playing.'

'Didn't you hear the bell?'

'No, miss,' said Carol with wide-eyed innocence.

'Sorry, Mrs Power,' said Merle.

'If anything like this happens again, you'll all be in detention,' Mrs Power said. She was quite nice as teachers go, but it was a wonder that she'd ever qualified. She believed any story you cared to tell her, however far-fetched. Green as cat sick, she was, and we all made the most of it.

I followed the rest into school, looking out for Beverly all the while. There was no sign of her, until Mrs Power opened the classroom door. There she was, sitting in her usual seat ahead of us.

I slipped into the seat beside her. 'How did you do that?' I said.

'Easy,' she answered. 'I ran round the back and used that entrance. It's quicker.'

I glanced round the class. They were looking at Beverly in pained surprise, as if they couldn't quite believe she'd managed to get past them.

Carol said, in a menacing whisper, 'See you after school then, suckers.'

Beverly started to tremble again.

'Why didn't you say something back there in the playground?' I asked her.

'I couldn't,' she said.

'Well, you're for it now,' I answered, not bothering to spare her feelings. 'They'll get you for sure. Me too, most probably.' I was scared too, but at least I wasn't shaking. I decided it must be awful to have a body that gave you away all the time.

'What can we do?' Beverly asked.

'How should I know? It isn't really my problem.' It was my problem though, I could see that. I was stuck with being Beverly's ally and protector whether I wanted to be or not.

'What shall we do at break?' she asked.

'Stay in, I guess. It's safer indoors than out.'

All through French, I wondered if it was too late for me to change sides again or not. OK, I could look at myself in the mirror without the monster face peering back now that I wasn't being mean to her all the time, but I was really starting to think it wasn't worth it. And then I remembered Patience, and how she would feel about me if I didn't defend Beverly in her hour of need. So I was caught between everybody; on the one hand, Carol and Co. would get me if I went against them, and on the other, Patience would disown me if I didn't.

The rest of the day was just like the one before. I couldn't concentrate on anything for dreading half-past three and having to face Carol and the rest of them. As soon as the bell signalled the end of afternoon school, I grabbed hold of Beverly's arm and we tried to slip out of the classroom under the protection of Mr Exton, but he wasn't having any of it. He wheeled round and said, 'Didn't you hear the bell? It means I am now a free man. I needn't see another tiresome child before nine o'clock tomorrow morning, so clear off to your homes, the pair of you, and let me get off to mine.'

'But –' Beverly began.

I pinched her quickly. There was no point in prolonging this. We were on our own now. 'Back way,' I said, and we started to run.

'Won't they guess we're going that way?' whimpered Beverly.

I just gritted my teeth and kept on running, with

Beverly lolloping clumsily behind the way she always did. And then, just as the gap in the fence was within reach, Carol sprang out from behind the rubbish bins, followed by Jess and Merle.

'Well, look who it isn't,' Carol said.

'And no teachers to act as guard dogs either,' added Jess.

I didn't dare look at Beverly. I knew she'd be wetting herself. Even I was shaking, though I was determined not to show it. 'Leave us alone,' I said. 'Exton's right behind.'

'No he isn't, he told you to get lost,' said Carol triumphantly. 'Now you'll both get what you deserve.' She nodded to Jess, who reached out and snatched Beverly's bag from her shoulder, tipping the contents on to the ground. 'Look at this. Half a packet of crushed crisps. A leaky biro. Tonight's homework and . . . what's this then? I don't believe it. A fluffy little doggy poo.' Jess drew out a pink fur dog about eight centimetres high. I glared at Beverly. How could she come to school with a thing like that? It was such an embarrassment it just wasn't true.

'Give it to me,' Beverly said in a loud but whiny voice.

'No,' said Jess, and she held it just out of reach.

'A doggy poo for a doggy do,' said Carol.

I must admit, I started to laugh.

Carol said, 'Even your cousin thinks it's funny.' Then she looked at me and said, 'Do you really want to hang out with her for the rest of your natural life? No one else will want to know you.'

It was true. I almost switched sides again. But before I could answer, Jess said, 'They deserve each other. They're all alike, those Oswalds. I mean, look at that gross grandmother they've got. Great fat bottom in tight orange trousers – colours clashing all over the place. And those stupid silver boots. She's just sad, and these two aren't any better. They've got as much style as Sooty.'

I just stood there with my hands clenched at my side, trying not to cry. I wanted to stand up for Patience, but no words came. Tears appeared suddenly and slid the length of my nose before blobbing on my shirt. The wet patch was clearly visible. I prepared myself for the cry-baby taunts that were bound to follow. Then suddenly, Beverly came to life. She lifted her head and looked each of them straight in the eye. They could say what they liked about her, it made no difference, but as soon as they started to mouth off about Patience, she was full of rage. She sprang forward as if she was going to wallop Jess, but instead she faced her calmly and said, 'And I'll tell you something, Jessica Vaughan. You think you're so clever, but you're a gutless wonder. You never do a thing without making sure you can hide behind Carol if the going gets tough.'

'Rubbish!' said Jess, looking taken aback.

'You're just cowards, the lot of you. You only pick on people who can't defend themselves, you're pathetic.'

'We're not,' said Carol, but I thought I heard her faltering.

'And you're nothing, nothing at all. You think you're so big, but it's all a load of monkey-nuts. You could be clever if you ever bothered to use that brain of yours, but instead you just keep acting the fool. You're not funny, you're just . . . you're just plain silly.'

Beverly was starting to get breathless with a mixture of fear and excitement. For a moment, I was afraid she'd fizzle out, but she kept on going. Now that she'd got started, it was as if it was hard for her to stop. 'And you Merle, you're the worst of all,' she said, her voice nearly at yelling pitch.

'*Me?*' asked Merle in astonishment.

'Yes, you. You know that what the others do is wrong, but you're too scared to back down. That makes you worse in my book. At least they don't know any better.'

'You're sad,' said Carol, but her voice lacked conviction.

'You know what? The only sad people round here are you lot. You've picked on me ever since I've been here and I've had enough, right? Any more and I'm going straight to Mrs Harcourt.'

'If you go you're dead,' said Carol, but her voice was so quiet it was almost a whisper.

'If I don't go I might as well be dead for all the life I'm having.'

'No one will believe you,' Carol answered.

Beverly stood her ground. 'They will, they know what you're like.'

'It'll be your word against ours. One against four.'

'Two against three,' I said quickly, before I had time to change my mind. I felt so sad. It was over. I couldn't be one of them any more, I'd lost my last chance. I was an outcast now, with only Beverly for company.

Merle was looking worried, but then that wasn't unusual for her. But Carol and Jess were looking worried too, and it was then that I knew that Beverly had beaten them – they wouldn't be bothering her any more, at least, not like before. Everyone fell silent.

Carol looked lost for once. Jess seemed angry and deflated, like a toddler who's just had a tantrum but failed to get its own way. Merle was plain embarrassed. She knelt down to tie her shoelace, hiding her face from the rest of us. I don't know how I seemed then. I only know that I felt really stupid. I'd been on the wrong side all along.

It was the first time I'd ever seen Beverly acting cool. She turned around and walked towards the school gate, slowly and calmly. I began to follow.

'You're finished, Grace!' called Carol.

I just ignored her and went on walking after Beverly. As I reached her side, I saw that she was shaking now. Her cool was gone and she looked as if she was going to cry.

'What's the matter?' I asked. 'You've done it, haven't you? You've got them off your back.'

'I'm not upset, I'm relieved,' she said.

We went on walking towards the High Street. I thought I might buy a cassette or something to keep me company now that I was about to have about as many friends as a skunk without a deodorant. I wished things could have been different. I would go back with my mother, I decided. It would make life easier. Then I thought of Patience. Along with my mother, she was the person I cared about most in the whole world. At least she hadn't found out about the way I'd treated Beverly. I still had that much left.

Beverly had stopped shaking now. She was looking excited. 'I told them what I thought of them,' she said.

I nodded.

'I did it,' she repeated, as if she couldn't believe it herself.

'Do you want to come to the music shop with me?' I asked. I wanted to put a stop to the gloating. Any minute now she'd decide she was invincible and goodness knows what that could lead to.

But to my surprise, Beverly didn't realize how honoured she should have been to get my invitation. 'No thanks,' she said, 'I want to get home. Mum and I are going out tonight. We haven't been able to go for months because of her illness.'

'Suit yourself,' I said frostily.

Beverly was obviously going to. She scarcely even said goodbye to me before she loped off home.

I watched her go, feeling really mad with her. It was me who'd told her to stand up for herself, and I was the one who'd backed her when she'd said she'd tell Mrs Harcourt. I'd practically saved her life and now she was running off home as if I hadn't done anything at all. The ingratitude of some people was beyond belief.

I mooched into the music shop. At the far end, in the classical section, there was a big cardboard cut-out of my mother standing over a stack of her CDs. Normally I would have felt quite proud, but instead I just felt miserable. I'd be back with her soon, spending most days and nights by myself apart from the babysitter. It wasn't a life I wanted any more.

I stood staring at the figure. I wanted to knock it over and watch the CDs clatter to the floor. Then suddenly, a voice said, 'Hi, Grace.' I turned round slowly. It was Merle. 'I told Carol and Jess that if you went to Mrs Harcourt it would be three of us against two. So I'm finished as well, I guess.'

I gave her a huge grin. 'Come and help me choose a tape,' I said.

Twenty-two

When I got home, Patience was in the kitchen, cutting potatoes into chips for the evening meal. Marley was going ballistic in the corner. On the worktop above him, just out of reach, were two large plaice. 'You could give him a little piece,' I said to Patience.

She smiled at me. 'I knew you'd go soft over Marley in the end,' she said, but she didn't offer him any of the fish. She was a lot harder than I was.

'How was school?' she asked me.

'OK. Same as usual,' I said, though it hadn't been, of course.

We went and sat at the kitchen table and listened to the spitting sound of frying fish and chips. 'How's Beverly?' Patience asked. 'Is she settling down again OK?'

'I don't think there'll be any more problems,' I answered.

'You mean the bullying's stopped?'

'I never said there was any bullying,' I replied quickly.

'You didn't have to,' Patience said. 'You know, Bev's all right once you get to know her. It's true that she doesn't take a big interest in clothes – her mum and dad can't afford to buy her much anyway – but that isn't everything, is it? And she's a little slower than you are, but we don't all do things at the same pace.'

'She laughs funny.'

'Well, you don't laugh enough, but I don't hold that against you.'

Marley was pawing at my lap. I picked him up and began to stroke him. His purrs almost drowned the sound of the fish and chips. It was cosy, sitting there. I was so comfortable that my eyes almost closed. And suddenly, I wanted Patience to know what I was really like. Then she could hate me and I could hate her back and return to my mother and forget she ever existed. 'It was me who was giving Beverly a hard time,' I said, forcing out the words.

I didn't look at Patience, but I could feel her looking at me. 'I know,' she answered.

'How? Did Beverly tell you?' I demanded.

'No, she didn't have to, I worked it out for myself. I'm not senile yet, you know.'

I sat with my fists clenched. Then I pushed Marley to the floor. He went down with a yowl of indignation. I was waiting for the lecture. I knew that Gran would shake her head sadly and express her disappointment. She'd then move into the shouting stage and tell me what a nasty person I was. Then finally, we wouldn't speak at all, except that every now and then she'd say how relieved she'd be when my mum came and took me back to live with her.

But all that happened was that Patience took the

fish and chips out of the pan and put them on warmed plates. Then she brought them to the table. She smothered hers with tomato ketchup, took a large mouthful and smacked her lips. 'No more talk of diets, Grace,' was all she said, but her tone was tense, and I could tell that she was trying really hard not to be angry with me.

I tried to eat, but my throat was too tight. Slowly, the tears began to roll down my cheeks. I wanted her to shout and yell; it would be less unnerving than this calm version of Gran. Patience was never calm.

'Go on then,' I said. 'Tell me how terrible and mean I've been. Go on!'

'I don't need to tell you, you already know,' she replied, still in that rather forced, calm voice.

'I hurt Beverly, your favourite grandchild. Aren't you going to start shouting at me?'

'So I shout. What does it change?'

'It would make me feel better!' I yelled, and I began to sob noisily.

'All right!' Patience shouted. 'You've been a hateful, selfish, miserable girl ever since you arrived, you've made Beverly's life an absolute misery and you're lucky I didn't pack you off back to your mother. How's that? Feel better now?'

'Yes!' I shouted back, the tears still running down my cheeks. At least she was behaving normally. At least she was treating me like a real person, a proper member of the family. She'd have shouted at Beverly all right if Beverly had done it. I was tired of having guest status. I wanted to belong. 'Patience, *please*,' I said. I could hardly get the words out. 'I'm . . . sorry,' I blurted. I'd never apologized to anyone before, and it was pretty frightening. My knees began to shake and I couldn't look at Gran.

There was a terrible silence. Then, suddenly, Patience gave a deep sigh and ambled over to my side of the table. She enveloped me in a big bear hug and said she still cared about me, and no matter what I'd done, I'd always be special to her. In that moment, I knew she had forgiven me and it was like coming home.

Patience got me to dry my tears. She made me a pot of tea and thin slices of toast to help me to eat. Then she sat with me and talked to me and held me for hours. And at last I could see that Patience loved me just as much as she loved Beverly.

Two weeks later, we were on our way to the station. For once, Patience said we could get a taxi, so me and Beverly sat squashed up against our gran as we meandered through the London traffic.

I didn't know why I'd asked Beverly to come. It had just seemed right, somehow. She was honking away with Patience, who was laughing a lot at her jokes. There's an old saying: 'If you can't beat them, join them,' so I got in there too, with stories about the people who came to see us when I'd lived with Mum. As she dabbed the tears of laughter from her eyes, Patience said, 'You know, you tell the funniest stories. You should write a book sometime, get them all down.' I smiled back at her, but I didn't say anything. I didn't think I was clever enough ever to write a book.

Victoria Station was packed. Beverly went off to get Gran a packet of sweets while we waited by the platform for the Gatwick train. I was so nervous I stopped being able to talk. When Beverly turned up, I was glad that she was able to keep up the chatter, it helped take my mind off things a bit. I wanted to see my mother, but at the same time, I was scared. I knew I'd changed. I was more grown up, somehow. I'd started to learn to think for myself and not rely on other people all the time.

And then, suddenly, there she was, hurrying along the platform in a deep blue coat, wearing a little hat and smart grey shoes. She looked smaller than I remembered her. 'Go and meet her,' said Patience, giving me a little push, and I started to move towards her, slowly at first and then faster and faster until I was running into her arms. 'Steady now, steady,' she said, as I almost toppled into her. She gave me a slightly disapproving look.

'Mum!' I gasped, hugging her tight.

She touched me lightly in return. 'You've grown,' she said. I was taller than her now.

I took her bag and started to gallop back to Gran.

'Careful, don't break anything,' my mother said. I wasn't sure if she meant my bones or the contents of the holdall I was carrying.

I was laughing and chattering with Beverly and Gran, while Mum watched us with that slightly critical look of hers. 'It's good to see that you've settled down so well,' she said, but in a way, I think she was disappointed that I'd begun to grow away from her.

We went to the same American diner we'd been to when I'd first arrived. Mum picked at a few French fries and a small veggie burger, while me, Beverly and Patience stuffed our faces with three large courses. I ate a pudding this time round. I even had a bit of Gran's.

'You won't be able to make such a pig of yourself when you come back home with me,' said Mum. There was a smile on her face, but I knew that she meant it. She always said 'You are what you eat'.

We all fell silent. I didn't know how to tell her.

'What is it?' she asked after a few moments.

I still couldn't say it.

'Go on,' urged Beverly.

'Mum,' I said, 'I think I'd like to stay here with Gran.'

It's been more than two years since I came to live in London. Mum visits whenever she can and me and Patience go a bit wild when we see her. She says it's like being attacked by a couple of whirlwinds, we never seem to stand still for more than a minute at a time. Mum thinks I've changed a lot since the day she first left me at the station. I'm full of fun now, she tells me, always ready for a laugh. Sometimes, I ask her what I was like before I came to live with Patience, but she doesn't really answer.

It was hard at school for those first few weeks after Beverly stood up to Carol and Jess, but at least there was Merle. I'd like to say that me and Bev are best friends now, but it isn't really true. She's family and we get on OK, but there's a barrier between us. Perhaps one day she'll trust me again, but Patience says it's no use trying to force it. I don't think Beverly's ever forgotten the way I treated her before, and I can't really blame her, I suppose.

We did set up a counselling scheme to help other kids who were being bullied. Patience helped, and Mrs Harcourt too, but it was our project, and it was up to us to deal with the problems. Grown-ups can't sort things out for you, not really. You have to find other ways.

I remember how much I wanted to be a counsellor. I thought it would be a way of being important and making friends. But in the end, it wasn't really about me, it was about the kids who were having a hard time. And although I saw one or two of them and tried to help sort things out, I wasn't the one kids turned to – it was Beverly. I suppose Bev knew more about trouble than I did. She was patient too, and she listened a lot.

I'm not a great listener. I guess it's because I've always preferred to do the talking. So when Patience said that someone should write about that time when I was almost twelve, I knew I didn't want it to be another Little Angel story. I wanted to tell it to you myself.